THE Colonel turned at last to face her, but he did not move away from the window, and the golden evening light behind him dazzled her so that she could not clearly see his face. In that low-pitched, shadowy room, against that bright background, his tall figure seemed for a moment to be charged with indefinable menace, and a little tremor of fear passed through her. Impatiently she shook it off, telling herself that she was being intolerably foolish.

"Have you never heard, Miss Tarrant," he said slowly, "that it is sometimes prudent to let a sleeping dog lie?"

The House at
Bell Orchard

SYLVIA THORPE

FAWCETT COVENTRY • NEW YORK

THE HOUSE AT BELL ORCHARD

Published by Fawcett Coventry Books, a unit of CBS Publications, the Consumer Publishing Division of CBS Inc., by arrangement with the Hutchinson Publishing Group.

Copyright © 1962 by J. S. Thimblethorpe

ISBN: 0-449-50006-3

THIS BOOK CONTAINS THE COMPLETE TEXT OF THE ORIGINAL HARDCOVER EDITION.

Selection of the Doubleday Romance Library

Printed in the United States of America

First Fawcett Coventry printing: December 1979

10 9 8 7 6 5 4 3 2 1

1

The Passer-by

The door of the house stood open, so that the light from within, mingling with that of the flambeaux which flared in the iron sconces flanking the entrance, spilled down the steps and over the coach waiting in the street. This was not one of the elegant town-carriages common enough in that modish quarter of London even in the early hours of the morning, but an old-fashioned travelling-coach, dusty and mud-splashed as though it had just completed a journey. Yet, in contrast to its travel-stained appearance, the four powerful horses harnessed to it were fresh to the point of restiveness; they pawed the ground and tossed their heads, impatient of the restraint imposed upon them by the grooms.

It was the incongruity of the scene which caught the attention of Sir Piers Wychwood as he walked by, for there was a sense of urgency about that dusty coach with its fretting team which seemed alien to the atmosphere within the house. A ball was obviously in progress there, for music came drifting faintly out into the warm summer night, and the open door afforded a glimpse of a spacious hall where liveried servants gossiped among themselves, their vigilance relaxed at this late hour when the stream of arrivals had ceased and the hostess long since abandoned her place at the head of the stairs.

Sir Piers knew the owner of that imposing house, and had, in fact, called upon him there only the previous day, but it was not that fact alone that halted him. He was essentially a practical man, yet something in the scene before him stirred his imagination. There was a hint of drama implicit in it. The play of light and shadow; the dark bulk of the coach with its driver huddled motionless in his seat; the gleaming coats and tossing manes of the horses; the distant music and the idling servants, all inspired in him an odd sense of expectancy. It was like a stage awaiting the entrance of the players, and a sudden, curious compulsion was upon him to see the play begin.

He halted just beyond the reach of the light, where the darkness seemed blacker by contrast, for he was convinced by the very nature of the scene that he would not be obliged to wait for long. Nor was he mistaken. After a few minutes the lackeys in the hall stiffened to sudden, statuesque silence, and a woman and two men emerged from the house. For an instant they paused on the threshold while one of the men spoke over his shoulder to someone within, but the unseen watcher was scarcely aware of him. It was the woman who captured and held his whole attention.

She was young, a girl in the elaborate finery of full balldress, over which a light cloak had been cast with obvious haste. Beneath it, a gown of pale-coloured satin shimmered in the torchlight as, with hooped skirts swaying, she came slowly down to the coach, and there were flowers in her powdered hair. Yet she moved as though in a trance, guided by one of her companions, her sweet young face frozen into a white mask of horror and grief from which her eyes stared as blankly as the eyes of a blind woman. To the man in the shadows there was something inexpressibly moving in the sight. The sense of incongruity investing the entire scene was sharpened and crystallized in the person of this unknown woman, in the bitter contrast between her festive attire and the stark tragedy in her face.

The stout old gentleman who held her arm handed her tenderly into the coach and then climbed in after her, while the tall master of the house stood looking into the vehicle's dark interior. Then the girl must have spoken to him, for he leaned forward in a manner which suggested that he had taken her hand in his own, and his answering words came clearly to Sir Piers in the shadows.

"My wife and I will follow you as soon as we are free of our guests. My poor child, I wish it were possible to go with you now, but be sure that we shall not be long after you."

He stepped back and signed to the waiting footman to put up the steps. The somnolent figure of the coachman stirred into life, the grooms sprang back from the horses' heads, and the coach lurched forward along the street, two outriders falling into place behind it. The man who had spoken stood looking after it, his tall figure outlined against the light behind him, which set a faint, glimmering halo about his gold-laced coat and powdered hair. Then he turned to enter the house again, and that same light fell for a moment across a dark, secretive face with bony features and deep-set eyes; the face of a man older than was suggested by his spare, vigorous frame and upright carriage. He passed into the house and the door shut behind him, and only the torchlight was left to illuminate fitfully the dark, deserted street.

The young man who had been a silent and unsuspected witness of that brief scene remained for several moments studying the unrewarding frontage of the house, and then he turned and walked slowly away, feeling that in some subtle yet indefinable way the past few minutes had been of profound significance. What connexion, he wondered, could there be between Colonel Fenshawe and the girl whose sweet, tragic face, glimpsed for a moment by flickering torchlight, had made so profound an impression upon him? She had the look of one lost and bewildered, stunned by a blow so brutal and so unexpected that the enormity of it could not immediately be grasped, and he was conscious of a desire, as compelling as it was illogical, to assure himself that she would find the comfort and protection of which she so plainly stood in desperate need.

He quickened his pace, telling himself impatiently that no man of sense would permit himself to be moved by a passing incident, a chance encounter which was unlikely ever to be repeated. The business which had brought him to London was infinitely more important than the troubles of an unknown girl, and it was with the failure of his errand and consideration of the next step to be taken that his thoughts should be filled, rather than with the memory of a woman's face. It was mere coincidence that she had emerged from the house of Colonel Fenshawe, where he had himself gone only yesterday in the vain hope of finding there some support for the purpose which had brought him from his native Sussex. The visit had achieved nothing, save a widening of the existing breach between the families of Wychwood and Fenshawe.

The Colonel, meanwhile, having re-entered his house, avoided the ballroom and salons where his guests were amusing themselves, and made his way instead to a study at the rear of the house. In that quiet room, where the sound of music penetrated but faintly, his elder son was standing by the window with a glass in his hand.

Harry Fenshawe was twenty-eight, with his father's

height and lean vigour and dark complexion, but with a greater degree of good looks than the elder man could ever have possessed. There was a suggestion of recklessness and self-will in his face, and more than a hint of a hasty temper. He was in riding-dress, his black hair unpowdered, his coat and spurred boots dulled by a film of dust.

"Well?" he said impatiently as his father came in, but the Colonel paused to close the door gently behind him before he replied. Then he said:

"Miss Tarrant has left for Richmond with the good magistrate. The shock of the news he brought was so great that it will be some hours, I think, before full realization of what has happened dawns upon her. By that time your stepmother and I will have joined her."

Harry continued to frown at him. "It might have been wiser if one or both of you had gone with her now."

"With the house full of guests?" Fenshawe retorted coldly. "That would scarcely be seemly, since, thanks to your obstinacy, we are not yet bound to her by any ties of kinship."

"Not yet?" Harry gave a short angry laugh. "Do you suppose we ever shall be, after what happened tonight?"

"I see no reason to doubt it," his father replied curtly. "Miss Tarrant finds herself alone in the world, in sore need of help and guidance which I shall do my best to provide, and of comfort, for which she can easily be persuaded to turn to your stepmother. Tonight's events, properly handled, cannot fail to draw her closer to us, and you could, if you wished, turn the whole situation to your own advantage. She is already more than half in love with you."

"God help her!" Harry retorted flippantly. He drained his glass and moved across to the table to refill it, adding more seriously: "For the last time, sir, I do not intend to marry Charmian Tarrant! Devil knows why you still try to insist upon it, when you might all this while have been arranging her marriage to Miles."

"You are well aware that her father, naturally enough, would not consider her marriage with my younger son while the elder is still unwed," the Colonel replied shortly. "Nor could I afford to alienate him by insisting upon it."

"Her father is dead!" Harry stood for a moment staring sombrely at the contents of the glass, and then swallowed them at a draught and reached out again for the decanter. His father's hand shot out to grip his wrist and he said sternly:

"Leave that! This is no time to be addling your wits with brandy."

"My wits are sharp enough!" Harry's voice was sullen, but he set down the glass and, breaking from his father's hold, moved away to the centre of the room. "Sharp enough, at all events, to mislike what happened tonight."

"I like it no better than you do," Fenshawe broke in coldly, "but there is no remedy for it, and nothing to be gained by quarrelling among ourselves. Your temper, Harry, is ugly enough even when you are sober, and I will not permit you to inflame it by drinking so that you may pick a quarrel with your brother as soon as he returns. Why in the fiend's name am I burdened with sons who are for ever at each other's throats? By God! I could wish you both a modicum of young Wychwood's level-headedness, irritating though it may be."

"Piers Wychwood?" There was a subtle change in Harry's voice, a sharpness, almost a hint of concern. "What the devil brings him into your mind?"

"The very good reason that what he conceives to be his duty brought him into my house yesterday. He is visiting his uncle, Lord Corham, in Hanover Square."

"Is he, b'Gad? And his duty, as he sees it, is to come carrying tales to you?"

"Tales?" Fenshawe repeated quietly. "What tales, Harry?"

There was a brief and, on Harry's part, somewhat awkward silence, while he obviously cursed himself for his hastiness. Then he said with a touch of bravado:

"How the devil should I know? If Piers considered it his duty to call upon you, 'tis certain it was not merely to pay his compliments. He has grown too damned respectable for my taste."

"That I can believe, your tastes being what they are," the Colonel replied acidly, "but do not flatter yourself that you were the object of yesterday's visit. He came to take *me* to task for neglecting my obligations, and wasting my substance here in London instead of looking to the conduct of my estate. Sir Piers takes his responsibilities as landlord and Justice of the Peace very seriously."

Harry laughed, on a note of relief which did not escape his observant parent. "I told you sir, that he has become confoundedly respectable since he inherited. Did he really have the impudence to criticize you?"

"He did, and vastly irritating I found it to be instructed in my duty by a man no older than yourself, and one, moreover, whom I have known since he was in leading-strings. Oh, he was courteous enough, but he left me in no doubt of the opinion he holds of me. If I spent more time at Bell Orchard, he suggests, the activities of Jack Godsall and his fellow smugglers there might be less blatant."

Harry, who had flung himself into a chair and stretched his long legs out before him, stared at his father for an instant and then threw back his head and roared with laughter.

"Oh, b'Gad!" he exclaimed. "I've heard it rumoured

that Piers wants to put an end to smuggling in our neighbourhood, but I never imagined he would be fool enough to attempt it. Why, there was a time when he liked nothing better than to help in running a cargo, and even now I have yet to hear of a few kegs of brandy or bales of silk being unwelcome at Wychwood Chase."

The Colonel, eyeing him with disfavour, showed no inclination to join in his merriment.

"There appears to be a good deal you do not hear of, Harry, even though you spend more time at Bell Orchard than any of us. Did you know, for example, that for the past two months Piers Wychwood has been doing his utmost to persuade the local Excise officers to take active measures against Godsall?"

Harry shrugged. "I know it! I know also that he might as well throw himself against a stone wall."

"Precisely, but do you know why he is so determined? It is not, as you seem to think, because he has suddenly become conscience-stricken at the thought of the illicit cargoes being brought ashore along our stretch of coast. He is convinced that Godsall is bringing Jacobite agents into the country along with his contraband."

The laughter faded from Harry's face and his black brows drew together in a frown.

"This is merely suspicion," he said slowly. "There has been talk of strangers coming ashore from the *Pride of Sussex*, but I'll swear no one has any proof of it."

"Give thanks that they have not," his father replied curtly, "and see to it that no one acquires any, least of all Piers Wychwood. He was obliging enough to tell me that the purpose of his visit to London is an attempt to stir the authorities here to action, since he has failed to do so in Sussex. He wants them to make an investigation into this alleged Jacobite activity."

Harry was sitting erect now, gripping the arms of his chair, plainly disturbed by this piece of information.

"Was he successful?" he asked curtly.

"I believe not. His comments upon the indifference of the appropriate officials leads me to suppose that he met with little encouragement. The truth is, of course, that with Prince Charles just across the Channel there are rumours of so many plots that none are credited without substantial evidence. If Piers could produce that, it would be a very different matter. He is a man of sufficient standing for his word to carry considerable weight."

"I do not like it!" Harry got up and began to move restlessly about the room, the frown still darkening his brow, his lips tightly compressed. "This could not have happened at a worse moment. Suppose Miles cannot discover what became of Rob Dunton after he left Richmond tonight? Dunton is a known Jacobite agent, and if he were taken, he might turn King's evidence out of sheer malice. Damn Piers Wychwood and his confounded high-mindedness! Why must he choose this time of all others to start stirring up trouble?"

He broke off, checked by the Colonel's swift, warning gesture, for footsteps were approaching the study door. A moment later it was opened, and Miles Fenshawe came into the room.

He was dark, like his father and elder brother, but there the resemblance ended, for Miles was of medium height and slender, graceful build. His handsome features had an almost feminine delicacy, and his air of fashionable languor contrasted strongly with Harry's restless vitality. His dress, too, emphasized the difference between them, for where Harry's riding-clothes were well-cut but plain, owing their air of raffish elegance more to the wearer's physical qualities than anything else, Miles was dressed in the height of fashion, his scarlet riding-coat and snowy buckskins covered by a flowing, silk-lined cloak which fell almost to his heels, and his point-edged hat set carefully upon the ordered curls of a powdered wig. The younger Mr Fenshawe was very clearly a dandy.

"Well?" Harry spoke sharply, a trace of anxiety sounding again in his voice. "Did you find Dunton?"

Miles shook his head, his dark eyes mocking as they studied the speaker's face. The antagonism of which their father had spoken was unmistakable, and even the most casual observer could not have failed to realize that these brethren were bound by few ties of fraternal affection.

"No, dear brother, I did not!" Miles' voice was a high-pitched, lazy drawl, deliberately affected. "I sought our Jacobite friend in every kennel, and could glean no news of him. He has covered his tracks well, wherever he has gone to ground. It is of no importance! Although it would have been more satisfactory to find him, he can do no great harm."

"No harm?" Harry repeated indignantly. "The fellow knows the truth, or enough of it to make a shrewd guess at the rest."

"And by whose fault does he know it?" Miles asked with lazy malice. "Not by mine, dear brother! Not by mine!"

"Peace, the pair of you!" their father interrupted curtly. "You plague each other like two schoolboys instead of grown men. Miles is right! Dunton cannot betray us without betraying himself, nor will he make any move against us until he has accomplished the mission upon which the Prince sent him to England. That will take precedence over all else."

"And when it is accomplished, sir?" Harry asked bitterly. "Are we to spend the rest of our lives with the knowledge that Rob Dunton has the power to ruin us if he can find the means to use it? That is a prospect which I, for one, do not relish."

Miles helped himself to brandy. "For once, Harry, I am inclined to agree with you," he remarked. "We shall all sleep more soundly when Dunton has been found and silenced. The only obstacle appears to be that we have no idea where to seek him."

"Precisely!" Colonel Fenshawe signed to him to fill another glass, and when he had done so, took it from him and sat down. "Therefore we must persuade him to come seeking us."

The brothers exchanged a puzzled glance; Miles said slowly: "May I inquire, sir, how you propose to do that?"

"Very simply. Dunton is known to the Government as an active supporter of the Stuarts, and therefore can make no accusation against us in person, but I am sure he will realize, as I have done, that there is one person who would have both the means and the will to destroy us, if she were put in possession of all the facts. I refer, of course, to Miss Tarrant."

Understanding dawned upon the young men. Harry gave a satisfied chuckle, and Miles said thoughfully: "You propose, then, to use Miss Tarrant as the bait in a trap?"

The Colonel nodded. "That is exactly what I intend. Your stepmother and I will leave for Richmond as soon as the last of our guests have departed, and you may be sure that we shall not permit Miss Tarrant to be parted from us again. It will seem natural for us to offer her guidance and protection at such a time. As soon as the funeral is over we will take her to Bell Orchard, for I believe that Sussex will be more convenient to our purpose than London. That, too, will occasion no surprise. Her father's suicide is bound to give rise to a deal of nasty talk, from which it will be our natural desire to shield her."

Harry was frowning again, and as soon as his father paused he said uneasily: "Bell Orchard? Is that entirely wise, sir?"

Miles laughed unpleasantly, but though the Colonel glanced sharply at him, he did not inquire the cause of his amusement. Instead he said:

"Are you thinking of Piers Wychwood's troublesome activities? We must be careful not to arouse his suspicions, of course, but otherwise I do not think we need trouble ourselves unduly. His efforts have met with singularly little success so far."

"What is this?" Miles asked curiously. "How does Wychwood enter into the affair?"

His father told him, briefly repeating what he had already said to Harry. Miles listened with a faint, mocking smile, and at the end said contemptuously:

"Our dear friend Piers! So earnest, so righteous—and so deplorably dull! I marvel that he could bring himself to leave his bucolic pursuits even to answer what he imagines to be the call of duty."

"Piers is no fool!" Harry said curtly. "What is more, I have never known him to abandon any project, once he has set his mind to it."

"I am inclined to agree with you in that," his father remarked reflectively, "but in this instance I feel that the advantages of carrying out our plans at Bell Orchard outweigh the risks. Wychwood is not likely to make Miss Tarrant's acquaintance, since her mourning will prevent her from taking any part in social activities."

"Oh, there are no sociable exchanges now between us and the Wychwoods," Miles put in maliciously. "Harry has seen to that."

"Indeed?" The Colonel's shrewd glance turned towards his elder son. "How is that?"

Harry shrugged, casting a furious glance at his brother.

"Merely a deal of fuss about nothing, sir. Piers saw fit to disapprove of what he chose to call my pursuit of his sister. Simply because I took the child riding without an attendant."

"The child, as you call her, is turned seventeen and remarkably pretty," Miles said softly. "Nor, as I heard it, were you engaged in riding when Piers discovered you."

"Piers is as eager to think the worst as you are to make mischief!" Harry retorted violently. "Damn it all, I did no more than kiss the girl!"

"It is fortunate that you did not," his father said cuttingly, "for I can think of nothing more likely to ruin us than to be forced into an unwanted alliance with the Wychwood family. So that was the tale you imagined that Piers had brought me!"

Miles laughed. "How foolish of you, dear brother!" he remarked. "I find Piers Wychwood insufferable, but even *I* know that he would not come whining to our father of such a matter. That is not at all his way."

"It most certainly is not," Fenshawe agreed scornfully. "Now understand me, Harry, for I shall not warn you of this again. I will overlook your indiscretions only as long as they involve women of a certain class. I will *not* permit you to trifle with innocent girls of good family such as Dorothy Wychwood. Nor am I prepared to wait indefinitely for you to show a proper obedience to my wishes. Miss Tarrant is approaching the day when she will become sole mistress of her fortune, and I do not intend to let such a prize slip through my fingers. While she is in mourning for her father there can of course be no formal betrothal, but before she leaves Bell Orchard, you will oblige me by reaching an understanding with her, not only to secure her money, but also to ensure that no word of our dealings with her father ever leaks out." He set down his glass and rose to his feet. "Now I must return to my guests. Remember what I have said."

He went out of the room, leaving Harry standing there with a dark flush in his cheeks and smouldering resentment in his eyes, resentment which flared into blazing anger as Miles said jeeringly:

"I have not heard him take that tone with you these ten years past! Thanks be to Heaven I am not the elder son."

In two swift strides Harry was beside him, towering over him, his face dark with fury.

"Liar!" he said between his teeth. "Where Charmian Tarrant is concerned you would give all you possess to stand in my place! Well, I am willing to step aside, but what would that avail you? You have been courting her for two years, and still she is scarcely aware of your existence."

Miles did not reply at once. He brushed past his brother and went to pour more brandy into his glass, standing by the table with his back to Harry.

"We all have our crosses to bear, dear brother," he drawled at length. "You are in danger of being bullied into matrimony by our confoundedly autrocratic father. Our stepmother is to be exiled to Bell Orchard to comfort the bereaved heiress—poor Lavinia, how she will hate it! And I? As you say, Miss Tarrant is scarcely aware of my existence." He sipped reflectively at the brandy for a moment, and then turned with lazy grace, the voluminous cloak swirling about him. He was smiling. "But she will be made aware of it one day, my dear Harry," he said softly. "Death itself is not more certain than that."

2

A Time for Tears

In the coach making its hasty way along the road to Richmond, Charmian Tarrant sat silent and unheeding, oblivious alike of the discomfort of that hurried journey and of the old gentleman beside her. She was frozen into a state of numb incredulity, her shocked mind refusing to accept the truth of the news which Mr Brownhill, her father's nearest neighbour, had so reluctantly brought.

Her thoughts went back to the events preceding this urgent journey, and the scenes unfolded in her memory with a clarity which as yet brought no pain, for they seemed to concern some person other than herself. She recalled the ballroom with its flowers and glittering chandeliers, and the shifting pattern of colour as the gaily-clad guests threaded the intricate movements of the dance. She had turned, laughing, to find Lavinia Fenshawe at her side, white with shock beneath the rouge, and had been led by her away from the music and the mirth to a quiet room where the Colonel and Mr Brownhill were waiting.

As gently as they could, they had broken the news that her father lay dead by his own hand, but Charmian had been unable to believe it. With mute disbelief she had allowed them to make what arrangements they chose, only rousing when she found herself in Mr Brownhill's coach and on the point of departure. Then, giving way for a moment to panic, she had frantically sought Colonel Fenshawe's guidance, and been reassured by the promise that he and his wife would join her as soon as they could. It was perhaps strange that she should turn for comfort to this man who had been her father's intimate for only two years, instead of to Mr Brownhill whom she had known all her life, but the Colonel was a man of strong character and commanding personality, beside whom the kindly, well-meaning old magistrate faded into insignificance.

Charmian Tarrant was an only child and an heiress; she was also a very lonely young woman. Her mother had died suddenly and tragically, in an accident nine years before, and her father, who had married late in life a lady many years his junior, had from that day withdrawn into an impenetrable aloofness. Always reserved and studious, with a deep interest in the past, he now immersed himself in his historical studies, and sought, by so doing, to ease the sting of his present sorrow.

Throughout Charmian's girlhood he had remained a kindly but remote figure, and only her deep affection for him had prevented her from revealing the resentment she often felt at their restricted way of life. She was a gentle and sweet-natured girl, but with spirit enough to rebel against the unexciting rhythm of her days. All their acquaintances were of her father's generation, and on the rare occasions when Charmian did attend some private party or local assembly, she did so in the care of Mrs Brownhill. This good lady was so conscious of the responsibility of chaperoning an heiress, and so terrified that her charge might fall into the clutches of some fortune-hunter, that she would scarcely permit the girl to leave her side.

Mr Tarrant was a wealthy man, and Charmian had inherited also a large fortune from a maternal uncle, and these facts, combined with a considerable degree of good looks, should have made it easy for her father to arrange for her an excellent marriage. He had made no attempt to do so, and as Charmian approached her late teens, the omission began to cause her a good deal of secret disquiet.

Matters might have continued thus indefinitely had not Mr Tarrant, on one of his occasional visits to London—excursions upon which it never occurred to him to take his daughter—made the acquaintance of Colonel Fenshawe. How and where they met Charmian did not know, nor what business they discussed at such length behind the closed door of her father's study whenever Fenshawe visited the house at Richmond, but she perceived at once that the Colonel was vastly different from the majority of her father's friends. He was first and foremost a man of fashion, in whose presence, in spite of his unfailing courtesy, Charmian felt acutely conscious of her lack of social experience, and her countrified dress manner. Through him she caught her first glimpse of a wider and more exciting world, and when, on his third visit, he brought with him his young, handsome wife, exquisitely dressed and overwhelmingly friendly, she responded to every overture with guileless eagerness.

Lavinia Fenshawe, it seemed, had resolved to take Miss Tarrant under her wing, and for the next few weeks Charmian lived in a whirl of excitement which culminated in her first visit to London. Her father, pleased to see her so happy, made no objection either to the visit or to the new and expensive wardrobe it required, and it occurred neither to him nor to his daughter that Mrs Fenshawe's kindness might be prompted by the fact that the Colonel had two unmarried sons of a former marriage, extravagant young men for either of whom the hand of an heiress would be a notable prize.

Charmian made the acquaintance of the younger of these two brothers as soon as she arrived in London, and Miles, enchanted by her soft brown eyes and shy, sweet smile, and equally enchanted by the size of her fortune, lost no time in stealing a march on his brother and paying court to her in the most lavish style. But though Charmian found his admiration gratifying at first, and was grateful for his escort to balls and parties, it soon began to pall. She disliked his many affectations, his intense preoccupation with dress and all that was fashionable, and found it impossible to take him seriously.

When Harry Fenshawe put in an appearance, however, her reaction was very different, for he seemed the embodiment of every romantic dream she had ever cherished. His dark good looks, the suggestion of dare-devilry that clung about him, contrasting so strongly with his brother's studied languor, even the fiery temper of which she caught occasional glimpses, fascinated and excited her, and when Mrs Fenshawe hinted delicately at the possibility of a marriage to strengthen the bond of friendship between their families, Charmian felt that her cup of happiness was full.

Two years had passed since then, she was still waiting for Harry to propose, and lately had begun to doubt whether he ever would. It seemed that he was deliberately avoiding her. He had always spent a good deal of time at his father's estate in Sussex, but now, it seemed, he lived there permanently, or else arranged his visits to the London house so that they did not coincide with hers. With her twenty-first birthday in sight—an almost unheard-of age for a girl in her circumstances to reach not merely unmarried but unbetrothed—Charmian was beginning to feel desperate.

But now these doubts and fears were forgotten, driven from her mind by the appalling news of her father's death. There seemed to be neither sense nor reason in such a tragedy. Suicide was the last, hopeless resort of those driven to desperation by a crushing weight of ill-fortune, or by some intolerable grief, but her father was neither of these, and it seemed incredible that he should have ended his life by violence, self-inflicted. Why had he done it? Why?

The question throbbed tormentingly in her mind, deepening the sense of unreality, of the utter impossibility of such a disaster. The journey seemed interminable, and it was with a sense of profound relief that she realized the coach was jolting at last through the familiar gateway of her home. Now this nightmare would be dispelled, and sanity return to the world.

Mr Brownhill descended stiffly from the coach and turned to help Charmian to alight. A pale dawn was breaking behind the trees at the edge of the garden, and below the sloping lawns the river was veiled in mist, but lights were burning in the lower windows of the house. The door was opened for them by a servant whose normally impassive face bore the marks of shock and grief, and as Charmian stepped into the hall, another door opened and Mrs Brownhill, plump and motherly, came out to meet her. She looked pale and tired, and her eyes were reddened with weeping, but she came forward with outstretched arms to take the girl's cold hands in her own.

"Charmian!" she exclaimed brokenly. "Oh my poor, dear child, what can I say? This dreadful tragedy—" her tears overflowed again, so that she was unable to continue, and could only press Charmian's fingers tightly in token of sympathy.

Charmian looked at her, and then at the sad-faced servant and at Mr Brownhill, tired and kindly and concerned, and slowly the awful reality began to force itself upon her. In horrified denial of it, still trying to thrust it away and wake from the nightmare, she said sharply, her voice high and strained in the silence:

"My father! Where is he? I want to see him!"

Mr Brownhill laid a hand on her shoulder. His face was twisted with grief and pity.

"My dear child," he said unsteadily, "do not insist upon that. The nature of his injury—you would find it too harrowing."

Reality could be held at bay no longer. It pressed upon her from every side, in the unnatural silence of the house, in the pale, sorrowful faces of her companions, most of all in the pitying words which sketched a picture from which her imagination recoiled in horror. For a moment or two she continued to stare at the old man, and then with a broken cry buried her face in her hands. There was to be no awakening, and home was not the sanctuary she had expected, but the source from which the nightmare sprang.

Of what followed she afterwards retained no clear recollection. Mrs Brownhill presently got her to bed, and sat with her in her darkened room while the summer dawn gave place to a day whose bright beauty mocked at sorrow and bereavement. The old lady was bewildered and a little frightened. Charmian did not weep; after that one broken, protesting cry she scarcely uttered a sound, but lay staring before her with wide, blank eyes until she fell at last into an exhausted sleep. Mrs Brownhill slept, too, dozing uncomfortably in her chair, until roused by the sound of the door being softly opened. An elegantly dressed young woman looked into the room, cast a swift glance towards the bed, and then laid a finger to her lips.

Mrs Brownhill, still dazed with sleep and weariness, obeyed an imperiously beckoning hand and followed the newcomer out into the corridor. The lady drew the door of the bedchamber shut again and said in a low voice:

"I am Lavinia Fenshawe, ma'am. How fares my poor Charmian?"

"She is sleeping now," Mrs Brownhill replied in the same tone, "but she has been so quiet, so calm! It does not seem natural."

Lavinia nodded. "So it was when she left London, but the breaking-point will come soon, no doubt. Let her sleep while she may." She paused, studying the elder woman's tired face, and then added smoothly: "You, too, are in need of rest, Mrs Brownhill. I will take your place with Charmian now."

The old lady hesitated, for though she was almost lightheaded with fatigue, she felt oddly reluctant to hand over her charge to this stranger. Mrs Fenshawe was very handsome, but her pale, blonde colouring and light-blue eyes gave an impression of coldness, and there was a certain hard selfishness about her mouth. No fault, however, could be found with her manner, and Mrs Brownhill decided that the doubts she felt were merely the result of weariness and the shocking events of the previous night. She gave a murmur of assent, and went slowly downstairs to join her husband.

It was an hour or so later that Charmian awoke. For a few bewildered moments she lay still, conscious only of a heavy weight of foreboding, a sense of disaster which her familiar surroundings seemed to belie. Then, as recollection forced itself into her mind, she gave a stifled cry and sat upright. At once the bed-curtain was drawn aside and Lavinia stood looking down at her. Charmian stared back, seeing in her presence there confirmation of all the terrible memories and fears which were confusing her mind.

"Lavinia!" she whispered. "Is it true? My father—"

"Yes, it is true!" With a swift, graceful movement Mrs

Fenshawe seated herself on the bed and took Charmian into her arms, "My poor child, would to Heaven it were not! There, my dear, weep if you will. It is a time for tears."

A sob had broken from Charmian's lips at Lavinia's first words, and the tears which had seemed frozen within her flowed at last. She wept for a long time, to the point of utter exhaustion, and all the while Lavinia Fenshawe remained at her side, stroking her hair and murmuring words of comfort, while elsewhere in the house her husband set himself to discover the exact circumstances of Mr Tarrant's death.

These were simple enough. Mr Tarrant had remained in his study after the rest of the household retired, but this was his habit and occasioned no surprise among his servants. He was known to suffer from sleeplessness, and generally spent much of the night with his books or, in fine weather, walking in the garden, to which a door from the study gave direct access. About midnight, the other occupants of the house had been roused by the sound of a shot, and when in alarm and confusion they had sought the source of the disturbance found the study door locked upon the inside.

Receiving no answer to his calls, the butler had taken it upon himself to force an entry, and there, to their horror, he and his companions had found Mr Tarrant huddled at his desk, his shattered head resting upon an open book and his dead hand still clutching a pistol. There was no evidence of any disturbance; the garden door was locked and the key in its accustomed place in a drawer of the desk; the only mystery surrounding Mr Tarrant's death was the reason which had prompted it. Why should a man in his apparently comfortable circumstances take his own life?

That was the question foremost in everyone's mind, but

for Charmian an answer to it was forthcoming a few days later. It was the day of her father's funeral, and she was sitting with Lavinia in the drawing-room, beside one of the windows which looked out over the lawns towards the river. There had been a storm the previous night, and though the weather was still warm, a damp, grey mist lay over the garden and the sky seemed to be pressing upon the tops of the trees. To Charmian, the whole world seemed muffled and stifling; she had wept until she could weep no more, and now was conscious only of utter weariness and desolation.

At last the silence was broken by the sound of approaching footsteps, and Colonel Fenshawe came into the room with the lawyer who handled Mr Tarrant's affairs. The Colonel, who had dealt calmly and capably with all the sad duties arising from the tragedy, walked across to Charmian and stood looking down at her.

"My child," he said kindly, "there is something which Mr Prentiss wishes to say to you. Do you feel yourself strong enough to receive him?"

The brown eyes, heavily shadowed in her white face, lifted to meet his; she said in a low voice: "I am strong enough, sir, if you and Lavinia will stay with me."

"We shall do whatever you wish, my dear," he assured her. "I think you know by now that our foremost desire is to ease your burden for you as far as we may."

He took her hand and led her to where the lawyer was engaged in low-voiced conversation with Lavinia, who said kindly:

"Come, my love, sit here beside me. This is a sad ordeal for you, but I am sure that Mr Prentiss will explain everything as briefly as he can."

The lawyer hastened to agree, and then, Charmian having seated herself at Lavinia's side, he took the chair to which the Colonel waved him. Fenshawe himself remained standing beside Charmian, one hand resting upon the back of the couch on which she and his wife were sitting.

"You will no doubt be aware, my dear Miss Tarrant," Prentiss began, "that the matter upon which I must speak to you concerns your late father's Will." He paused to lay his hand on some documents he had placed on the table beside him, and Charmian bit her lip hard to stop its trembling. "Before I read it, however, there is something which I must endeavour to make clear to you. The Will was drawn up some years ago, when Mr Tarrant's affairs were in a vastly different state than they stand in today."

He paused again, and Charmian stared at him with knitted brows. After a moment she said in a low voice:

"I fear I do not properly understand you, Mr Prentiss. Papa's circumstances were as they had always been, were they not?"

Mr Prentiss seemed reluctant to reply. He took off his spectacles and polished them and then replaced them on his nose, looking at her over the top of them.

"Unhappily, my dear young lady, that is not so," he said at last. "It is my painful duty to inform you that your unfortunate parent found himself in grave financial difficulties. So grave, in fact, that there can be no doubt that they furnish the reason for this terrible tragedy."

Charmian put a hand to her head. "But that is impossible," she said dazedly. "Papa was a rich man."

The lawyer shook his head. "He was facing ruin, Miss Tarrant. Over the past two years he disposed of vast sums of money, against my advice and for some purpose which he refused to disclose to me. This house is heavily mortgaged, and even when everything has been sold, I fear that it will prove barely possible to satisfy all his creditors."

The words seemed to come to Charmian from a great

distance, and the lawyer's kindly, troubled face appeared to be floating before her eyes in a wavering mist. Mrs Fenshawe uttered an exclamation of concern and produced the smelling-salts which she had apparently kept in readiness, supporting Charmian meanwhile with an arm about her shoulders. After a few moments the deadly faintness passed, and Charmian turned her head to look up at the Colonel, saying piteously:

"I do not understand! How *could* Papa have lost all his money?"

"My dear child, it seems unlikely that that question will ever be answered," he replied, taking her hand and holding it reassuringly between his own. "We can find nothing among his effects to indicate how he disposed of his fortune. All we can do now is to settle his affairs to the best of our ability, and that sad business you may safely leave to Mr Prentiss and to me. It is not fitting that you should be troubled by it."

"This is a grievous blow to you, Miss Tarrant," the lawyer put in compassionately, "though there is some consolation to be found in the fact that you are still amply provided for under the terms of your late uncle's Will. When you reach your twenty-first birthday, which event I believe to be imminent, his entire fortune will pass into your hands." He sighed and shook his head. "That is a grave responsibilty for a young woman to bear alone."

"I am sure, Mr Prentiss," Fenshawe said smoothly, "that Miss Tarrant's affairs will be safe in your hands and in the hands of the present trustees of her uncle's estate. Meanwhile her friends must exert themselves to look after her, and to give her what comfort they can." He looked again at Charmian. "My dear, this has been a great shock to you. I think you should let Mrs Fenshawe take you to your room."

Charmian nodded wearily. Her head ached, and her

tired mind refused to grapple with the mystery which had just been laid before her, for it was a riddle too hard for her to read. She allowed Lavinia to lead her to her bed-chamber, and was persuaded to lie down upon the bed. Mrs Fenshawe, sitting beside her, said quietly:

"Charmian, my love, how would you like to come with me to Bell Orchard for a time? You need a period of quiet and a change of surroundings to help you to recover from this shocking affair."

Charmian, who had been lying with closed eyes, opened them to look with profound gratitude at the other woman. Her first thought was that Harry was at Bell Orchard—she knew nothing of his visit to London on the night of her father's death—and he was the one person above all others for whose presence she longed. Colonel Fenshawe and his wife were kind, but their kindness was expressed in practical ways, in ministering to her physical needs or dealing with the grim duties arising from her father's death. They could not give her the solace she craved, and seemed unaware of her crying need for strength to which to lean, and for the deep, unspoken comfort which could come only with love and understanding. If Harry could give her these things, she would know that all was well between them, and would wait patiently for him to declare himself.

"How good to me you are, Lavinia," she said unsteadily. "I would like that above all things. Mrs Brownhill says that I may stay with her for as long as I wish, but I would so much rather go away from Richmond for a time. To remain here can only keep painful memories alive, and if this house is to be sold, I do not think I could bear to be by while it is done."

"That is settled, then!" Lavinia spoke briskly, hiding her own resentment. She detested the country, but was sufficiently well acquainted with her husband's plans to know that upon this occasion she would be given no choice in the matter. "We will leave for Sussex as soon as it can be arranged. You know, my child, that we feel ourselves responsible for you, since you have no relatives to take you into their care."

"There is only my Great-aunt Emmeline in Yorkshire," Charmian replied dispiritedly. "I *could* go to her, I expect, although I have never met her. She is very old, and has not left her house these ten years."

"Heavens, child, you do not want to bury yourself in the wilds of Yorkshire!" Lavinia exclaimed. "I know that you will be obliged to live very quietly while you are in mourning, but after that it will be high time to see you established in a home of your own. It is a thousand pities that you are not already married." She paused, narrowly regarding the girl's pale face, into which her words had brought a faint tinge of colour. "To be sure, this is not the time to be talking of a bridal, but there is no need, I believe, to make any secret of the fact that the Colonel and I hope one day to welcome you into our family. Remember that, my dear, and do not think of seeking shelter under any roof but ours."

3

The Sleeping Dog

So to Sussex they went, as soon as arrangements for the journey could be made, Charmian and Lavinia travelling in the Colonel's luxurious coach, and Fenshawe himself riding beside it. Charmian was glad to leave Richmond, the house where her father had died, and the spate of gossip which his suicide had provoked. It would be a profound relief to find herself in new surroundings, where none but the Fenshawes need know more than that she had been recently bereaved.

Being unused to travelling, and still suffering from the effects of shock and grief, she found the journey something of a strain, and was thankful when the first distant glimpse of the sea told her that they were nearing its end. Evening was falling over a fertile countryside of wood and meadow, and as the coach descended a gentle slope, Charmian saw away to their right a lazy river and the clustering roofs of a village, while on the crest of the hill beyond a great mansion loomed impressively against the sunset sky. That, she thought, must be their destination.

She was therefore a good deal surprised when, at the

next crossroads, the coach turned to the left, away from the village which Lavinia told her was called Wychwood End. Later Charmian was to learn that the house on the hill was Wychwood Chase, but on that first evening she felt no curiosity concerning it, but merely surprise that it was not the home of Colonel Fenshawe. This, it seemed, lay some miles farther on, but at last the coach turned from the road through a stone-pillared gateway, and after traversing a long, winding drive, came to a halt before the house of Bell Orchard.

It stood in a green hollow within sight of the sea, a modest manor house, old and rambling, with timbered walls and gabled roof; a picturesque place, certainly, but totally different from anything that Charmian had expected. The sunset light still lay golden upon the higher ground around it, but the house and its old-fashioned garden were already drowned in a deep lake of shadow. It seemed strange that Colonel Fenshawe, who was obviously so wealthy and whose London house was so large and impressive, should be content with this insignificant country residence.

Entering the house, Lavinia led her guest to a pleasant front-parlour which was apparently the nearest approach to a drawing-room that Bell Orchard could offer. The room was low-ceilinged, panelled from floor to roof, and small by the fashionable standards of that year of 1744, its furnishings in keeping with their setting. Lavinia stood in the middle of the room, untying the strings of her cloak and looking disparagingly about her, and Charmian, watching her, reflected irrelevantly that this room demanded sombre velvets and stiff brocades. Mrs Fenshawe in her flower-sprigged silk and vast, hooped skirt, her pale hair unpowdered beneath a beribboned hat, looked totally out of place in it.

The door opened, and every other thought was driven

out of her head as Harry came into the room. He kissed
his stepmother's hand and inquired civilly after her
health, and then turned to pay the same courtesy to
Charmian, adding a conventional expression of sympathy
for her loss. The formality of his words she could have
forgiven, attributing it to Lavinia's presence, but it was in
vain that she searched his face for some evidence of real
feeling, some indication that her grief touched him also.
He looked merely sullen, and she realized with a painful
flash of insight that he had come to greet her merely because good manners demanded it. He resented the necessity, and he resented her presence at Bell Orchard.

She had thought it impossible to experience a deeper
unhappiness than she already felt, but she realized now
how mistaken she had been. In that moment of bitter
truth she knew beyond all doubt that Harry cared nothing
for her, that if ever he asked her to marry him it would
be as a matter of expediency, because she was still a rich
woman, and because his father and stepmother were constantly urging him to it. Whether or not she could face
marriage on such terms she did not know.

Less than a week later her disillusionment was complete. Coming down from her room on a bright, summer
afternoon, and crossing the hall to the parlour door,
which stood ajar, she was halted within a yard of it by the
sound of low, furious voices—Harry's and Lavinia's—
within the room.

". . . a little courtesy to Miss Tarrant," Lavinia was
saying angrily. "You have spent barely an hour in her
company since we arrived. Is it too much to ask that you
forgo your vulgar amusements for a little while in the interests of us all?"

"Too damned much by far!" Harry replied bluntly.
"How long will it be before you and my father realize that
I am in earnest when I say I will not marry her?"

"Oh, I am out of all patience with you!" Mrs Fenshawe exclaimed. "At present you have only to crook your finger and the silly creature will fall into your arms, but that state of affairs will not last for ever, especially if you treat her in this off-hand way. Let me tell you, Harry, that I have not allowed myself to be burdened with that tiresome girl for the past two years just to stand by and see nothing come of it. In fact, had I not imagined that you would have her safely married to you within six months, I would never have befriended her in the first place. But it is all of a piece! You and Miles are the most selfish creatures alive! You and he together created this appalling muddle, and 'tis I who have to bear the brunt of it."

"Oh, have done, in the devil's name!" Harry said exasperatedly. "I know you detest Bell Orchard, but it is not my fault that you have to stay here. I was against bringing the girl here at all, but no heed was paid to me!"

Charmian waited to hear no more, but turned and fled blindly across to the open door and out into the sunshine. Never in her life had she felt so utterly humiliated. It was bad enough to know that Harry had never had any intention of marrying her, that he was weary of being plagued to do so, but Lavinia's words had shown her how transparently plain her own eagerness for the match had been. And what Mrs Fenshawe had seen, others must have seen also; half London must have been laughing at her behind her back. Nor was there any escape. She could not leave Bell Orchard without giving her reasons for doing so, and thus bringing even more humiliation upon herself.

For a while indignation sustained her as she walked through the gardens, and out of them into the small park which surrounded the house. Inland, this was bounded by the road leading to Wychwood End, but on the seaward side, the direction which Charmian had taken, there was no such definite boundary, and the parkland gave way almost imperceptibly to rolling dunes, and thence to the pebble ridge and sandy levels of the shore itself. She climbed to the crest of the dunes, over the soft sand and patches of rough grass, and stood looking out to sea, her black gown sombre against the brightness of the deserted, sunlit shore.

This was her first visit to the coast and as such had the attraction of novelty, but the emptiness of the scene before her brought fresh realization of her loneliness. Anger faded, to be replaced by a kind of weary despair, so that the bright prospect before her shimmered in a sudden mist of tears. The weight of misery and bewilderment which had pressed upon her ever since her father's death seemed all at once too heavy to be borne, and she could endure no longer the endless, profitless circle of her thoughts. She must speak to someone of her doubts and fears, seek an answer to questions which had tormented her ever since the lawyer told her of the disappearance of her father's fortune.

There was only one person to whom she could turn for advice, and that was Colonel Fenshawe. Though she saw him now, as she saw the rest of his family, for the opportunist he was, and knew that his kindness had been prompted merely by the desire to secure a rich bride for his son, there was no doubt that he had been on terms of intimate friendship with her father, and was familiar enough with the ways of the world to tell her whether or not the suspicion which for days had been growing in her mind had any foundation. Yet if she wished to seek his advice she must do so without delay, for she had heard him say that morning he would be returning to London on the morrow.

That evening she sought him out and requested the favour of a private conversation with him. He agreed at

once and, leading her to the library, asked how he could
be of service to her.

"Colonel Fenshawe," she said earnestly, "I have been
thinking a great deal about what Mr Prentiss told us
concerning Papa's affairs, and there is still much that I
cannot understand. My father was a man of moderate
tastes, and lived quietly, without extravagance of any
kind. He did not gamble or speculate. Yet he died at the
point of ruin, even though two years ago he was a rich
man. How could he have lost so much in so short a
time?"

The Colonel shook his head. "My child, that is a question which neither I nor any man can answer. Your
concern is natural, but there is nothing to be gained by
brooding over the mystery."

"You agree, however, that there *is* a mystery?"

"Only in so far as your father chose to keep his own
counsel. I have no doubt that there is a simple explanation, did we but know it."

"I must know it, sir!" she said desperately. "I shall
never be able to rest until I do. I have come to ask you to
help me."

There was a pause. The Colonel took out his snuff-box,
helped himself to a pinch, and then closed the box again
and sat looking down at the design on its enamelled surface. At last he said quietly:

"My dear Miss Tarrant, I realize that at present the recent terrible events occupy your mind to the exclusion of
all else, but it will not always be so. You are young, and
must endeavour to put this tragedy behind you. Whatever
reason your father had for disposing of his fortune, it is
plain that he did not wish you to know of it, or he would
have left some written explanation before he took his life.
There was no such document. I was with Mr Prentiss
when he went through your father's papers, and there was

not a single word among them to throw any light upon the mystery. I counsel you to leave it so."

Charmian shook her head. "Colonel Fenshawe, I cannot! Do you think I can go through life with that question unanswered? I have thought and thought, and only one explanation occurs to me. I believe that someone cheated Papa out of his fortune."

Again there was a pause. Fenshawe regarded her with an expression she could not read, for the frown in his eyes might have indicated perplexity, disbelief or even disapproval. Certainly he offered her no encouragement to continue, but she forced herself to do so even in the face of this apparent indifference.

"If that is so," she resumed at length, "it must surely be possible to discover who did so, and how it was done. I understand that you will shortly be returning to London. When you do so, I beg that you will inform Mr Prentiss of my suspicions, and ask him to do whatever he thinks necessary to discover the truth."

"To what end?" Fenshawe asked in a cold voice. "Even if what you suspect is true, I can see no way of discovering it."

"But Papa must have disposed of many thousands of pounds in the past two years. Such sums as that cannot disappear without trace."

"Perhaps not, but even if the money could be traced, and the identity of the supposed criminal established, what would you gain? It is out of the question that the money could be recovered."

"I never imagined, sir, that it could be, nor must you think that I am prompted by the desire for vengeance. But if such a criminal does exist, then surely it is our duty to try to expose him, and so save others from similar suffering?" She paused, studying his face with some perplexity, for he was still looking decidedly forbidding. She moved her hands in a helpless gesture. "It may be that nothing can be done, but I feel that I owe it to my father's memory to see that the attempt is made. If I write a letter to Mr Prentiss, will you see that it reaches him?"

Fenshawe did not reply at once. He got up and walked to the window, which offered, beyond park and garden, a distant glimpse of the sea, and stood there with his back to her for perhaps two minutes. It seemed that he was deliberating, and Charmian waited in silence and some trepidation for him to speak. It was not easy for her to persist in the face of his obvious disapproval, but she was stubbornly determined not to be turned from her purpose. Now that every other hope and dream was shattered, the solving of the mystery had somehow become the most important matter in her life.

The Colonel turned at last to face her, but he did not move away from the window, and the golden evening light behind him dazzled her so that she could not clearly see his face. In that low-pitched, shadowy room, against that bright background, his tall figure seemed for a moment to be charged with indefinable menace, and a little tremor of fear passed through her. Impatiently she shook it off, telling herself that she was being intolerably foolish.

"Have you never heard, Miss Tarrant," he said slowly, "that it is sometimes prudent to let a sleeping dog lie?"

Was it a warning, or a threat? The cold, quiet voice seemed to be the voice of a stranger, and not of the kindly man who had shouldered for her the burdens of the recent terrible days. Charmian pressed her hands tightly together, feeling the palms cold and clammy with an unnamed fear, but still some inner obstinacy drove her on.

"I want to know the truth," she replied flatly. "Perhaps I am wrong to disregard your advice, perhaps I appear ungrateful in not being guided by it, but I cannot rest until this mystery is solved."

"Then the truth you shall have," Fenshawe replied coldly. "For your own sake I have sought to keep it from you, but I cannot permit you to start an investigation which must inevitably have consequences more far-reaching than you can even imagine. Remember that, when you begin to regret your curiosity."

"You know the truth?" Charmian spoke in a tone of incredulous inquiry, and then added with growing conviction: "You have always known it!"

"Yes, I know it," he repeated dispassionately, and moved away from the window at last, and came to stand before her. "Are you aware, Miss Tarrant, where your father's political loyalties lay?"

She shook her head, staring at him in growing bewilderment. "He had no interest in politics."

There was irony in the dark, secret face confronting her. "You are mistaken, Miss Tarrant. He felt a deep and passionate loyalty to his rightful King, and a profound faith in the ultimate triumph of the Stuart cause."

Charmian rose slowly to her feet, one hand at her breast, her eyes wide and horrified.

"Are you trying to tell me, sir, that my father was a Jacobite?"

He inclined his head. "That is precisely what I am telling you. He was a Jacobite, as I am, and all my family. That was the interest we had in common, the shared loyalty which first drew us together."

She shook her head, still staring at him in patent disbelief. "I cannot credit it," she murmured. "All he cared about was his studies, the history he was preparing."

"A history of the struggle between King and Parliament," the Colonel agreed in a level tone. "Studies which traced the fortunes of the Stuart dynasty for over a century. Do you marvel that from these should arise a deep conviction of King James's unassailable right to the English crown and a desire to see the German usurper overthrown?"

Charmian dropped down into her chair again; she was trembling so violently that she could no longer remain standing.

"This is treason, sir," she said in a shaken whisper.

He shook his head. "In this house, Miss Tarrant," he replied grimly, "the only treason is sympathy with the Elector of Hanover."

Charmian made a small, incoherent sound of dismay and disbelief, and covered her face with her hands. She knew, of course, that there were still people in England who hoped for the return of the exiled Stuart king, and there had been talk of late that his son, Prince Charles Edward, with the aid and blessing of Louis of France, was planning an attempt to recover the throne by force of arms, but though she knew of these matters she had never concerned herself over them. The last Jacobite uprising had taken place eight years before she was born, and such things as treasonable plots and armed invasions seemed to have no place among the realities of life. Now, without warning, she found herself in the midst of such activities, and was asked to believe that her father had possessed similarly misguided convictions.

Fenshawe waited patiently for all the implications of what he had said to dawn upon her. He propped his shoulders against the shelves of books behind him, and once more took snuff from the gold and enamel box, shaking the lace ruffles back from his hand. At length, as he had known she would, Charmian raised her head, and asked the question for which he had been waiting.

"What has this to do with the loss of Papa's fortune?"

He shrugged slightly. "Your father, my dear, had been

convinced for years of the justice of the Stuart claim, but though he would willingly have done anything in his power to aid their cause, he had no notion how to set about it. All he could do, whenever he visited London, was to frequent the company of those who felt as he did, in the hope that one day some opportunity would offer itself. Eventually, his path and mine crossed."

He paused, and again took snuff, closing the box with a snap which sounded loud in the silence. Charmian, still huddled in her chair, was aware of the strong force of his personality, and found no difficulty in understanding how her studious, unworldly father had fallen so completely under its spell.

"I will not weary you," Fenshawe resumed, "with all the details of our ripening acquaintance. It is sufficient to say that eventually your father; finding in me one who was prepared to do more to aid the Cause than merely drinking loyal toasts and railing against the Elector, confided to me his desire to give some practical aid, and asked how he might do so." He shrugged again. "His years prevented him from taking any active part in our work, but there is one thing of which we are always in desperate need, and that is money. With that he was plentifully supplied and he gave it generously. Too generously, as subsequent events have proved." He paused again and then added deliberately: "That is where your father's fortune went, Miss Tarrant—to aid his rightful King. It could have been spent in no more noble cause."

She moved her hands in a protesting gesture. "But to ruin himself, and then take his own life! That is to carry any loyalty to the point of madness!"

He sighed. "Ah, that I did not foresee! His exact resources were unknown to me, and I had no suspicion until after his death that he had placed himself so deeply in debt. Had I known it, I would naturally have used every endeavour to dissuade him." He moved away from the bookshelves and came to set a hand on her shoulder. "Your father, Miss Tarrant, was a very brave man," he said gravely. "He might, perhaps, have weathered the storm and salvaged something from the wreck of his fortunes, but there was always the danger that suspicion might be aroused and the rest of us implicated. He took the only course he could think of to prevent such a disaster. It would not be too much to say that he gave his life for his King."

Charmian did not reply, and once again silence descended upon the room. Fenshawe moved quietly away and went to stand again by the window, but with his back to it this time so that he could watch the girl. He wanted her to have time to think over what he had said, to realize all its subtle implications, and to regret, as he felt certain she would, the persistence which had provoked his disclosures. There was still a little more to be said, and soon the right moment would come to say it.

For perhaps five miuntes he stood there, watching the different emotions which were mirrored in her face, and then, judging that the time was now ripe, he went forward again to stand beside her. She looked up with a start, as thought she had forgotten his presence.

"It is natural," he said, "that you should be disturbed, perhaps even shocked, by what I have told you, but you will perceive, I am sure, that I cannot afford to have any inquiry made into your father's private affairs." He paused, and then added in a voice charged with meaning: "*Any* inquiry!"

She stared at him in puzzlement which was only the beginning of alarm, and said in a faltering voice: "I do not understand."

He smiled, but it was neither pleasant nor reassuring. "I think you do, my dear," he said softly. "A little consideration will make plain to you, if it is not already obvious, that by telling you what I have, I place the lives and fortunes of numerous people in your hands. Now it may appear to you to be your duty to inform the authorities of these matters." He paused to look inquiringly at her, but she made no reply, and only stared at him with frightened, fascinated eyes. He shook his head. "Do not attempt it, Miss Tarrant! We all regard you with affection, but nothing—nothing, you understand—must be permitted to endanger the Cause for which we work. Try to forget all that I have told you this evening. Believe me, it will be far better—for you—if you can!"

4

The Meeting

There was a storm blowing up from the north-west, and the day, which had been hot and bright, was becoming rapidly overcast. Sir Piers Wychwood, riding homewards to Wychwood Chase, cast a knowledgeable eye at the great bank of purple-black clouds sweeping across the sky, and urged his horse from a trot to a canter. The storm was likely to be violent when it broke, and he had no desire to be caught by it in the open.

He was returning from a visit to the house of General Sir Percival Grey, a few miles westward along the coast, during which he had tried to enlist the old gentleman's support in his attempts to put an end to what Piers felt certain was a dangerous and treasonable traffic between the exiled Stuarts and their supporters in England. As before, he had met with no success. He had no proof to offer, and without it the General, like other local landowners, was not disposed to interfere in the smuggling which had been profitably carried on along the coast for generations. Everyone took advantage of it; many of the smugglers were respected members of the community, and if there was a rougher element among them which occasionally gave rise to crimes of quite appalling violence, that was all the more reason not to incur their ill-will. The local Excisemen seemed incredibly apathetic, and even fiery old General Grey, glaring at Piers from beneath bushy white brows, had hinted irritably that he was making a mountain out of a very small molehill.

Piers had an uneasy suspicion that the General had expected him to broach a very different subject—in short, to offer for the hand of his grand-daughter, Miss Selina. (Piers' sister Dorothy maintained that Selina herself had been expecting it for years.) It would be an eminently suitable match, even though Miss Grey, a lady of high principles and a decided turn of mind, was twenty-five years old and of a disposition which was at times a little less than amiable. She was well-born and well-dowered, and as practical and level-headed as Piers himself. There were no frivolously romantic notions in Selina's neat, dark head; if Piers offered for her she would accept him, since he was the most eligible bachelor in the neighbourhood, and she would be a dutiful wife and a capable mistress of his household.

It was all so very suitable that Piers himself did not know why he still held back from the final, irrevocable step. It was high time he married. Better, perhaps, to do so now, and forget the suspected Jacobite conspiracies in which no one but himself seemed particularly interested.

Forget, too, that memory which for weeks had haunted him with a persistence of which he was a little ashamed, the memory of a girl's white face in the torchlight. In vain he had tried to erase it from his mind, and he found himself constantly indulging in idle, profitless speculation concerning her. Had she found comfort in her hour of trouble? By what name was she known, and what did she look like when she smiled?

Finding himself thus unprofitably engaged once more, he uttered an exclamation of impatience, and urged his horse briskly up the long, gentle slope of the hill which lay between him and the gates of his home. He reached its crest, and before him the road swept down in a long curve past the gates, to disappear a short distance beyond into the belt of woodland which lay between Wychwood Chase and the village half a mile away. Ahead of him, about half-way down the slope, a coach was travelling in the same direction, driven in a way which showed more regard for speed than for safety. It was an elegant vehicle of polished wood and gleaming paintwork, drawn by a team of powerful bays, and Sir Piers had no difficulty in recognizing it as the property of Colonel Fenshawe.

He frowned, and slackened speed again, for he had no doubt that the coach contained Lavinia Fenshawe, whom he disliked intensely. He had heard, somewhat to his surprise, that she was staying at Bell Orchard. Her present haste, like his own, was probably due to a desire to reach home before the storm broke, and if he overtook her before she had passed his gates, common civility would compel him to offer her shelter at the Chase until it was over.

So he checked his horse and waited in the shadow of an overhanging tree, and as he watched the swaying, lurching carriage ahead of him, that importunate memory returned again. He had only to close his eyes to see the girl as vividly as he had seen her that night outside Fenshawe's house, with her shimmering gown and powdered hair and sweet, grief-stricken face. What the devil ailed him, that he could not put her out of his mind?

The coach was level with the gates; it was past them; in a few moments it would be out of sight among the trees and he could ride on again. It was jolting wildly over the ill-kept surface of the road, and even as Piers prepared to move forward, the off hind wheel struck a large, protruding stone and was wrenched off, to go bounding away into the tall grass on the far side of the road. The coach lurched crazily on to its side and came to rest at a precarious angle in the ditch, only prevented from overturning completely by the hedge-crowned bank beyond. The horses plunged and reared in a panic which the coachman was unable to control, and the groom, flung from his place by the impact but apparently unhurt, scrambled shakily to his feet and stumbled towards them, showing a fine disregard for the occupants of the carriage.

Piers set spur to his horse and plunged headlong down the hill towards the scene of the accident. Drawing rein beside the wrecked coach, he leaned from the saddle to wrench open the door, and then sprang to the ground as Mrs Fenshawe appeared in the aperture. She was considerably dishevelled, her wide straw hat tilted at a ridiculous angle, and though her face was white, it soon became clear that this was due more to anger than to fright. She allowed Piers to help her down from her precarious perch, but once safely on the ground turned from him with scarcely a word of thanks to vent the full force of her fury on the unfortunate servants.

A faint sound from within the coach caught Piers' attention, and with a startled glance at the unheeding Mrs Fenshawe he set a foot on the wheel and swung himself up to look into its interior, to find there the huddled, dark-clad figure of a second woman, who appeared to be trying to raise herself from the far corner, where the thorny branches of the hedge protruded through the shattered windows. Assuming this to be Mrs Fenshawe's maid, and reflecting that it was characteristic of that lady to have forgotten her, he made haste to go to her assistance.

Broken glass splintered beneath his feet as he slid rather than stepped down the sloping floor of the coach, but he steadied himself by gripping one of the leather straps and got his free arm round the woman's waist, hoisting her to her feet. She clutched at his coat, saying in a dazed murmur:

"What happened? Oh, my head!"

Her voice was soft and well-bred, certainly not the voice of a waiting-woman, and Piers realized that it was not a servant but a friend whom Lavinia Fenshawe had so callously abandoned.

"The coach lost a wheel, ma'am, and ended in the ditch," he replied reassuringly. "Do you feel equal to being helped down on to the road?"

"I—I think so," she faltered. "I struck my head, and was knocked senseless for a moment."

She lifted her face towards him as she spoke, and the black silk hood slipped back from disordered, light-brown hair. For the first time he could see her clearly, and it was with a distinct sense of shock that he found himself looking down into the face which had lingered so vividly in his memory. He was astonished, and yet beyond astonishment was the curious feeling that this meeting was inevitable, and had been so ever since the moment he first saw her in London. Such odd fancies did not usually trouble the practical mind of Sir Piers Wychwood, and once again he wondered impatiently why this girl should have so strange an effect upon him.

"Charmian!" It was Lavinia Fenshawe's voice, petulantly inquiring, indicating that she had at length remembered her companion. "Charmian, are you hurt? Pray, Sir Piers, tell me what is amiss!"

"One moment, Mrs Fenshawe! Your friend is a good deal shaken," he replied, and looked down at Charmian with a smile. "You will be out of here in a trice, ma'am, and then you will feel a great deal better. Come, let me help you!"

He assisted her to reach the doorway, and saw her aided to the ground by Mrs Fenshawe and the groom, who had at length been prevailed upon to leave his horses. Lavinia, apparently anxious to make amends, clasped the girl in her arms.

"My poor child, are you sure you are not hurt? I vow I am the most heartless wretch alive to neglect you so!"

Charmian, who, besides a blow on the head, had sustained the shock of being flung into a corner of the coach with Mrs Fenshawe's substantial weight on top of her, was in fact feeling considerably bruised and shaken, but managed to summon up a faint smile.

"It does not matter, Lavinia, and I am not hurt, truly I am not. It was as great a shock for you as it was for me."

Lightning flickered above the hill behind them, and a rumble of thunder echoed her words. Piers, who had jumped down and gone to look at the horses, now returned to the two ladies and said briskly:

"Mrs Fenshawe, the storm is almost upon us and I fear there is no time to reach the Chase, but if you will condescend to come to the lodge, my people there will be glad to offer you shelter. Your servants can lead the horses up to the stables, and see to it that as soon as the storm is over, one of my carriages is made ready to convey you home."

Lavinia looked at her wrecked coach and then at the threatening sky, and realized that she had little choice. She disliked Piers Wychwood quite as much as he disliked her, looking upon him as a slow-witted country squire with no social graces, but the only alternative to his suggestion was to trudge the half-mile to the village and probably be drenched with rain before she got there. She inclined her head with frigid courtesy.

"You are very kind, sir, and we will do as you suggest. Come, Charmian!"

She swept past him with as much dignity as the situation permitted, and started back along the dusty road towards the lodge, leaving Piers torn between amusement and annoyance. He found this grand manner ridiculous, since not five minutes before she had been railing like a fishwife at her servants. Charmian had obediently followed her friend, and Piers delayed only long enough to issue a few brief orders to the coachman and groom before hurrying after the ladies.

As he came up with them, Charmian stumbled and nearly fell, and he put out a hand to steady her, looking with some concern at her white face.

"I fear you are still feeling considerably shaken, ma'am," he said in his deep, pleasant voice. "Pray take my arm."

She did so with a murmur of thanks, and leaned gratefully upon it, for her head throbbed and she felt more than a little dizzy. Lavinia was walking a yard or two ahead and Charmian could not see her face, but did not need to do so to know that the elder woman was still in a furious temper. The situation savoured slightly of the ridiculous, and that was something Lavinia could not endure.

A few drops of rain pattered down, heralds of the approaching storm, and without looking round Mrs Fenshawe quickened her pace. Charmian would have done likewise, but Piers said calmly:

"Do not disturb yourself, ma'am. We have only a few yards to go and the storm is still a little way off. We shall reach the lodge before the rain becomes heavy."

She realized that what he said was true, for though the hiss of the rain could be clearly heard as the storm swept down the valley towards them, the imposing gates of

Wychwood Chase were now close at hand. She glanced
up at her rescuer, really looking at him for the first time,
for hitherto the only thing about him which made any impression upon her was his kindness, and the reassuring
calm of his manner.

He was a young man, tall and broad-shouldered, with a
pleasant but somewhat serious countenance. There was a
good deal of resolution in the firm lips and square chin,
and the expression of the blue-grey eyes was extremely
level and direct. His fair hair was drawn severely back in
a ribbon, and his attire of brown cloth coat, buff breeches
and gleaming top-boots almost austere in its plainness.
Yet he had an air of quiet assurance which could come
only from wealth and breeding, and there was some qual-
ity about him, a kind of serene strength, which Charmian
found oddly comforting. The thought passed fleetingly
through her mind that this was one man upon whom it
would be safe to rely.

When they reached the lodge they found that Lavinia
had already gone inside, but the lodge-keeper was at the
door to meet them, while his wife made Mrs Fenshawe
free of the tiny parlour. Both husband and wife were considerably flustered, a state of mind which Lavinia's dis-
dainful air did nothing to dispel, but the arrival of Sir
Piers soon caused a calmer atmosphere to prevail.
Charmian, seeing how with a word and a smile he set the
couple at their ease, and observing the obvious affection
with which they regarded him, could not help contrasting
this with Bell Orchard, where servants seemed to be either cowed or intolerably insolent.

Lavinia, belatedly recalling the demands of etiquette,
formally introduced Sir Piers to Miss Tarrant, before inquiring, with a civility which failed to mask complete indifference, after the health of his mother and sister. He
assured her that both were well, and thereafter they

chatted with careful politeness upon topics of general interest. Charmian took no part in the conversation, but was glad to lean back in her chair and close her eyes, only half-attending to what was being said.

The rain was now lashing furiously about the little house, and lightning and thunder followed each other almost continuously, and Mrs Fenshawe, after some ten minutes of courteous but laboured conversation, left her chair and went to stand by the window, watching the violence of the storm. Piers remained leaning against the table in the middle of the room, and thoughtfully studied Miss Tarrant, who was still sitting with closed eyes. The significance of her black gown, relieved only by a narrow edging of lace about the neck, and a deeper fall of lace where the sleeves ended, was not lost upon him, and although the shocked bewilderment he remembered so vividly had faded from her face, the marks of a deeper and more enduring sorrow had succeeded it. He read it in the shadowed eyes and drooping lips, in the overwhelming sadness of her whole countenance as she sat, unaware of his regard and so totally unguarded, before him.

The storm, for all its violence, was comparatively brief, and barely half an hour passed before the sky grew lighter, the downpour slackened to a drizzle and then stopped, and the sun began to break through the drifting clouds. Charmian opened her eyes to find the little parlour full of light, and Sir Piers' gaze fixed with unexpected intentness upon her. She flushed and sat upright, lifting a hand to her disordered hair, aware of a confusion which was not altogether unpleasant.

It was not long before they heard the sound of approaching hooves and wheels, and the lodge-keeper's wife came to tell them that the coach was at the door. Lavinia gave a mere condescending nod as she swept past her and

out of the house, but Charmian paused to smile at the
woman.

"Thank you for letting us shelter in your house," she
said in her soft, gentle voice. "It was very kind."

Out of the doors the air was indescribably sweet, for
though the tattered remnants of the storm-clouds were
still drifting away seawards, and the drip and trickle of
water could be heard on every side, the sun was already
drawing sweetness from flowers and grass and rain-soaked
earth. For some reason Charmian's heart lifted with pure
pleasure, the first happiness she had felt since her father's
death, and she said impulsively to Piers, who had followed her from the house:

"How beautiful everything is now! It almost makes the
storm worthwhile."

"Charmian!" Lavinia, already in the coach, spoke irritably. "Come along, child, and do not stand there in the
mud! Let us get home, in pity's name!"

Charmian started guiltily, and then suddenly the ab-
surdity of the anti-climax struck her, and she gave a little
gasp of laughter. As Sir Piers handed her up into the
coach, her eyes met his for an instant, and she saw in
them a rueful amusement that matched her own. The
memory of that moment of shared laughter stayed with
her as the coach bore her away, and she found it curiously comforting. No one at Bell Orchard, she reflected
with faint surprise, seemed to laugh very much except in
malice.

Piers stood watching the coach until it disappeared into
the woods, and then, after a few words with the lodge-
keeper, he mounted his horse and rode thoughtfully up
the hill along the avenue of splendid chestnut trees.
Wychwood Chase was a stately building, rather less than
a hundred years old, with terraced gardens upon either
side, and an impressive entrance fronting the broad sweep

of gravel before the house. Piers handed over his mount to the groom who was waiting there to receive it, and went quickly up the graceful flight of steps to the front door of the mansion.

He found his mother and sister in one of the smaller drawing-rooms. Lady Wychwood sewing and Miss Dorothy idly fingering the keys of the spinet. Her ladyship, a dignified, grey-haired woman of middle age, with the same firm mouth and blue-grey eyes as her son, looked up with a smile as he came into the room.

"So you are home again, Piers," she said as he came to kiss her hand. "Surely you did not ride through the storm?"

"No, I have been at the West Lodge," he replied. "Mrs Fenshawe's coach met with an accident at our gates just as the storm broke, and I took her and her friend to the lodge for shelter. There was no time to bring them here."

"Praise be!" Dorothy put in mischievously as he paused. "Mrs Fenshawe always makes me feel like a milk-maid—blowsy, buxom and bucolic!"

Piers chuckled, but Lady Wychwood shook a reproving head.

"This liveliness, my love," she told her daughter, "is a tendency you should strive to check." She turned to Piers. "Was the accident a serious one?"

He shrugged. "Serious enough, but fortunately no one was much hurt. I fancy that Mrs Fenshawe's dignity, and consequently her temper, suffered more than anything."

He gave them a brief description of what had happened, and concluded by saying to his mother: "I think it would do no harm, ma'am, for you to call upon Mrs Fenshawe. I have had some differences with the Colonel, but I understand that he has now returned to London, and it will not do to be upon bad terms with our neighbours."

He glanced at his sister, still seated at the spinet. "Take Dorothy with you."

Dorothy looked up, her blue eyes wide with surprise. "You said I was to have no more to do with the Fenshawes!"

"I said that you were to have no more to do with Harry Fenshawe," he corrected her, "and I have not changed my mind on that score, I promise you. There is no reason, however, why you should not go to Bell Orchard with your Mama. I should like you to make the acquaintance of Mrs Fenshawe's friend, Miss Tarrant, who, so I understand, suffered a tragic bereavement a few weeks ago."

Dorothy made a little grimace, raising her brows and pursing her lips, and ran fingers across the keys of the spinet to produce a mocking, tinkling ripple of melody. Lady Wychwood said mildly:

"If the young lady is in mourning, Piers, it is not likely that she will be receiving company."

He had been regarding Dorothy with a faint frown, but at that turned back to his mother.

"In ordinary circumstances I would agree with you, but I have a curious impression that the circumstances are not ordinary. Moreover, Miss Tarrant appears to be alone in the world, since if she had relatives she would scarcely be staying with Mrs Fenshawe at such a time, and if she is treated with no more consideration than was shown her this afternoon, her situation cannot be a happy one."

Lady Wychwood looked puzzled. "Do you mean that she finds herself, as it were, in the position of a poor relation?"

"No," Piers replied slowly, "for she was dressed as fashionably as Mrs Fenshawe herself, and appeared to be upon terms of equality with her. But, knowing that household as I do, I cannot imagine her receiving a great deal of comfort or sympathy there." He laid his hand on the back of her chair, looking down at her with a smile. "Will you do this for me, Mama?"

She still seemed slightly puzzled, but returned the smile and reached up to pat his arm.

"Of course, my dear, if you wish it. I will go to Bell Orchard tomorrow."

Dorothy, still coaxing a lilting melody from the spinet, had apparently lost interest in the conversation, but her eyes were thoughtful, and presently, when Piers had gone out of the room, she jumped up and ran with a swirl of petticoats to seat herself on a low stool at her mother's feet.

"Mama!" she exclaimed breathlessly. "Piers seems to be excessively interested in this Miss Tarrant. Do you suppose—?"

"I suppose nothing, my love," Lady Wychwood replied firmly, "and neither must you. You are too fanciful, Dorothy!"

"But how wonderful if she could divert his mind from Selina Grey," Dorothy persisted, "for you know, Mama, that you have been as worried as I have that he might offer for Selina. I vow I have been in a quake of fear ever since he rode out this morning, in case that was the reason for his visit to General Grey."

Lady Wychwood sighed. "Selina is an admirable young woman," she said despondently, "but I will own that I have not the smallest desire for her to become my daughter-in-law. But it is your brother's concern, Dorothy, and not yours or mine. We must not make any attempt to interfere."

"Well, *I* would interfere very happily if I thought it would do the least good," Dorothy reported. "Piers is the dearest brother alive, and I *do* want him to be happy. And that he could never be if Selina were here, poking that long nose of hers into everything—"

"Dorothy!"

"But it is long, Mama! You know it is, and she is for ever prying into other people's concerns and trying to make them behave as *she* thinks they should, and saying spiteful things about them in that horrid, self-righteous way she has. Oh, it would be too dreadful if Piers married her!"

"We do not know yet that he has any such intention."

"Why else would he go so often to call upon General Grey?" Dorothy demanded bitterly. "Mama, we *must* prevent it, and if becoming acquainted with Miss Tarrant is the way to do so, then I, for one, will spare no pains to be kind to her. To be sure, I cannot imagine our sober, practical Piers doing anything as adventurous as falling in love at first sight, but he does seem excessively concerned about her."

"Dorothy, you must endeavour to conduct yourself with more propriety," Lady Wychwood protested. "You have no business to be talking in this fashion. Moreover, when you meet Miss Tarrant, you may like her no better than you like Selina Grey."

"No one could be worse than Selina," retorted her irrepressible daughter. "I am sure I shall like her very well, and so will you. Why, the accident to Mrs Fenshawe's coach was the greatest good fortune imaginable! Just wait and see if I am not right!"

5

Wychwood Chase

Lady Wychwood was as good as her word, and the next day saw her carriage making its way down the long, winding drive to Bell Orchard. Dorothy, seated beside her mother, had already convinced herself that her brother's concern for the unknown Miss Tarrant betokened an interest far deeper than their brief, casual meeting justified, and was dwelling gleefully on the disappointment which this would cause the detested Selina Grey. Dorothy had a shrewd suspicion that it was Selina who had carried tales to Piers of his sister's liking for the company of Harry Fenshawe, and she would not readily forgive this deliberate sowing of discord between her and Piers. The incident had provided a foretaste of what might be expected if Selina became Piers' wife, and Dorothy felt that she would go to any lengths to prevent such a thing.

Lavinia Fenshawe was by no means pleased when her butler announced Lady Wychwood and her daughter, but succeeded in hiding her feelings. She welcomed the visitors graciously, made Miss Tarrant known to them, and assured her ladyship that she had recovered completely from the shock of the accident.

"Though it was my poor Charmian who suffered most," she added lightly, "for I was flung quite on top of her, and the poor child struck her head a severe blow. But Sir Piers came most gallantly to the rescue, and made all right in a trice, did he not, my love?"

Charmian nodded, and looked with a shy smile at Lady Wychwood. "He was very kind," she agreed. "I am exceedingly grateful to him."

Her ladyship regarded her kindly, for her first impression of Charmian Tarrant was a favourable one. "I am happy to think that my son was at hand to offer his assistance," she replied. "Is this your first visit to Sussex, Miss Tarrant?"

Charmian's eyes clouded. "Yes, it is," she said in a low voice. "I lived in Richmond until—until my father died."

Lady Wychwood uttered a civil expression of sympathy and tactfully turned the conversation to other topics, and Mrs Fenshawe responded eagerly. She seemed unwilling for them to speak of personal matters, and though this might have been prompted by a desire to spare Miss Tarrant's feelings, Dorothy did not feel that this was the case.

She remembered Piers saying the previous day that he felt the circumstances of Miss Tarrant's presence at Bell Orchard were not altogether ordinary, and, for Dorothy, this was more than enough. She had a vivid imagination and a tendency to let it get the better of her, so that she was for ever dramatizing the most commonplace incidents, and seeing mystery and drama where neither existed. Having already cast Charmian Tarrant in a romantic rôle, it was not difficult to picture her as the victim of some sinister plot, from which it would, of course, be necessary for Piers to rescue her. The fact it might be exceedingly difficult to persuade her practical and level-headed brother to enter into the adventurous spirit of such an undertaking was something which, for the present, Miss Wychwood was disposed to ignore.

It was obvious, however, that she would be carrying out his wishes by establishing a cordial relationship with Miss Tarrant, so she made every effort to be pleasant to her, and followed this up, as she and her mother were leaving, with an ingenuous suggestion that perhaps Mrs Fenshawe and her guest would care to visit them at Wychwood Chase in the near future. Lady Wychwood, who had found Miss Tarrant sufficiently to her liking to wonder secretly whether there was any foundation for Dorothy's outrageous suggestion the previous day, at once confirmed the invitation, but Mrs Fenshawe, giving Charmian no chance to speak, said quickly:

"It is most kind of your ladyship, but since Miss Tarrant is in mourning, it cannot be thought proper for her to go into company."

"My dear Mrs Fenshawe, I would not dream of suggesting that she should," her ladyship replied in shocked tones. "There can be nothing amiss, though, in you and her spending an hour or so with us one day, if you would care to do so."

"Oh, Lavinia, may we not go?" Charmian said eagerly. "I do not wish to seem lacking in respect for Papa's memory, but I would so much like to accept Lady Wychwood's invitation."

Mrs Fenshawe realized that she was fairly trapped. To persist in a refusal would seem churlish, and might even arouse unwelcome suspicion if Lady Wychwood mentioned the matter to her son. With a smile which successfully masked seething anger, she said lightly:

"Of course, my love, if you feel yourself equal to paying calls we can most certainly go. You know that I am willing to do anything that will give you pleasure."

It was arranged that the visit should take place three
days later, and as the time approached, Charmian realized
that she was looking forward to it with an eagerness out
of all proportion to so small a diversion. This was not
merely because she had taken an instant liking to the
Wychwoods, or even because she was lonely and unhappy
at Bell Orchard. At the back of her mind, like a threatening shadow darkening all her days, was the thought of the
disclosures which Colonel Fenshawe had made to her before returning to London. These had profoundly shocked
and frightened her, and raised in her mind numerous
unanswerable questions. Was there any real danger to the
peace and security of England in the activities of which he
had spoken, or were he and his associates deluding themselves into believing that they could further a cause already lost? Was it her duty, in spite of the Colonel's
veiled threats, to inform the authorities of what she had
been told? Would they believe her, and what punishment
would she suffer at Fenshawe's hands?

It seemed to Charmian that every attempt she made to
solve her problems merely created others, more formida-
ble than those which had gone before. The things which
Fenshawe had told her cast a new and sinister light upon
his desire to see her married to his son. Her father's fortune had been swallowed by the insatiable demands of the
Stuart cause; was her own destined to go the same way?
Harry might be firm in his refusal to marry her, but she
could not forget that he had a brother, who had already
proved to be her most persistent suitor. If the Colonel
failed to browbeat his elder son into marriage, he might
well do all in his power to make her the wife of the
younger.

It was in vain that she reminded herself that the ultimate decision, now that her father was dead, rested with
her alone. Her present situation offered no encouragement

to such thoughts, and she began to sense a devious purpose behind the suggestion that she should visit Bell Orchard. She felt herself isolated there, cut off from the few friends she had. She had written to Mrs Brownhill soon after her arrival in Sussex, but had received no reply; now it was plain that Lavinia was averse to her striking up a friendship with the Wychwoods, and that knowledge fostered in Charmian a desperate determination to pursue the acquaintance at all costs. She was growing increasingly certain that danger of some kind lurked at Bell Orchard, and she must have friends to turn to in case of need.

The day chosen for their visit to Wychwood Chase was warm and bright, thus depriving Lavinia of any excuse not to go, and this put her into an ill-humour at the outset. She complained incessantly as they drove along the dusty road, past farm and cottage and into Wychwood End. Crossing the old stone bridge that here spanned the sleepy river, they left the village behind them and presently passed into the shade of the woods. Here the road began its gradual ascent of the hill, and soon they were passing the scene of the accident and entering the avenue of chestnut trees. Charmian's thoughts went back to the last time she had seen this place, and she found herself wondering whether Sir Piers would be at home that day. Apparently Lavinia's thoughts had been led along similar lines, for she remarked peevishly:

"Heaven grant we are spared young Wychwood's company this afternoon, for though I can occasionally tolerate his mother and sister, him I find unendurable at any time! I do not know why I allowed myself to be persuaded into this visit at all!"

"Why do you dislike him so?" Charmian asked curiously. "I thought he was most kind."

"Kind?" Lavinia gave a short, angry laugh. "What

kindness is to be found in that sort of patronizing civility? The trouble with Sir Piers, my dear Charmian, is that he can never forget for an instant that he is Wychwood of Wychwood, the great man of these parts. He fancies that gives him the right to ride rough-shod over everyone, and has the impertinence to look down upon any who do not conform to his narrow, countrified standards of behaviour. Oh, I detest the man, and there's an end to it!"

Charmian said no more, but she thought she now had the answer to the puzzle of Mrs Fenshawe's dislike of Sir Piers. It had its roots in jealousy and resentment. The Wychwoods were undoubtedly the most important local family, and that was galling to anyone who, like Lavinia, must always hold the centre of the stage. Even more galling must be Sir Piers' very evident lack of interest in her as a woman. In London she was always surrounded by admirers; she thrived on masculine admiration, and it must be infuriating that the only personable young man within reach, outside her own family, should remain unmoved by her charms.

When they reached the house and were conducted to the drawing-room, they found only Lady Wychwood and her daughter awaiting them. Mrs Fenshawe was clearly relieved, but Charmian, responding to her ladyship's warm welcome and Dorothy's eager greeting, was conscious of a feeling of disappointment. She overcame it, and forced herself to take part in the somewhat stilted flow of conversation, but Dorothy soon began to show signs of restlessness. Presently, when Charmian commented politely upon the exceptionally fine views afforded by the elevated position of the house, she jumped to her feet and said impetuously:

"Yes, but they are much finer from the terraces! Come outside with me, Miss Tarrant, and I will show you."

Charmian accepted this invitation eagerly, paying no

heed to Lavinia's look of disapproval, and followed Dorothy out into the sunshine. There were three terraces upon either side of the house, and Dorothy, choosing those which looked towards the coast, led the way to the balustrade bordering the highest level.

"Bell Orchard lies yonder," she remarked, "though we cannot see the house itself, even from here, because it stands in a hollow."

Charmian followed the direction of her pointing hand, and frowned. "There?" she repeated in astonishment. "I supposed it to lie much farther to the left."

Dorothy laughed. "That is because the road curves in-land to cross the river at Wychwood End," she explained. "You had to travel nearly four miles to get here, but in reality the two houses are little more than a mile and a half apart. There is a shorter way between them, a bridle-path which leads down through the woods to a ford, and then continues across Colonel Fenshawe's land. The river marks the boundary between the two estates from a point half a mile above the ford to the sea."

"I see," Charmian said slowly. "Yet at Bell Orchard we are much closer to the sea."

"Yes, that is because of the line of the coast. Some-times in winter, when the weather is stormy and the wind blowing from the sea, it seems almost as though the house were on the shore itself. I do not think I would care to live there."

They were walking along the terrace now. Charmian said casually: "You have known Colonel Fenshawe and his family for a long time?"

"Yes, all my life, though not as well, of course, as my brother knows them. He and Harry Fenshawe were close friends as boys. They are the same age, you know, and they went to the University at the same time and then made the Grand Tour together."

"Oh?" Charmian could not conceal her surprise, for she would not have supposed that a serious young man like Sir Piers had much in common with Harry Fenshawe. "I did not realize that there was such a degree of intimacy between them."

"Well, there is not, nowadays," Dorothy replied frankly. "The Fenshawes are in London a great deal, and we have not lived there since my father died, so naturally we all meet less often. Mrs Fenshawe does not care for Bell Orchard, or for our quiet country ways, but, of course, you are aware of that."

"Yes," Charmian agreed in a low voice, "I am aware of it." She paused, considering her next words. "Forgive me, Miss Wychwood, but I have the impression—a mistaken one, perhaps—that there is an awkwardness, almost an antagonism between the two families. Pray do not think that I am prying into matters which do not concern me, but I am in constant dread of doing or saying something which may give offence in one quarter or another."

There was a pause, and then Dorothy said slowly: "Yes, I can understand that you should feel it to be so, for there *is* a coolness between us. My brother holds strong views upon the duties of a landowner towards his estates and his tenants, and he is occasionally very outspoken. He and the Colonel have disagreed more than once on that score."

They had reached the steps of the terrace and descended to the lower level before she spoke again. Then she said abruptly, as though having had some difficulty in reaching the decision to speak at all:

"I had better be completely frank with you, Miss Tarrant. A little while ago Piers quarrelled very violently with Harry Fenshawe, and I was the cause of it. I suppose I did behave thoughtlessly, but there was no harm in it— after all, I have known Harry since I was a baby. But

Piers can be prodigiously strict at times, and when he found us alone together, he said that Harry was not a fit person for me to associate with and I was to have no more to do with him. I had never seen him so angry, for in the ordinary way he is the most even-tempered man alive. Harry, of course, has a quite dreadful temper, and I thought that they were going to come to blows there and then. However, they did not, but that was the end of any semblance of friendship between them. I must say it seems foolish to end it so, for such a paltry reason."

Charmian, listening to this artless recital, found that it did not pain her as it would have done only a short time before, though it puzzled her a good deal. If there was this coolness between the two families, why were the Wychwoods exerting themselves to offer friendship to her? Was Sir Piers' absence today an indication that, in doing so, his mother and sister were going against his wishes? The thought caused her to feel a totally illogical pang of dismay.

"I trust," she said carefully after a moment, "that your brother does not, for that reason, look with disfavour upon this visit to his house by Mrs Fenshawe and myself. I would not wish to be the cause of any further differences between you."

Dorothy gave her irrepressible chuckle. "My dear, there is not the least likelihood of that! It was Piers himself who suggested that Mama and I should call upon you the other day. He hopes, I think, that you and I may soon become friends, and, for my part, I should like to believe that he is right."

"I hope so, indeed!" Charmian replied earnestly. She did not pause to question Sir Piers' motive for desiring such a friendship. It could not be the same as Colonel Fenshawe's, since he could know nothing whatsoever of her circumstances. "The truth is, Miss Wychwood, that my friends are very few."

She tried to speak lightly, but the effort was not altogether successful, and on a sudden impulse Dorothy caught the other girl's hand in her own.

"I am sorry," she exclaimed, "but you must not feel that now, you know! I am sure that we are all going to be the best of friends."

"Are we?" Charmian halted and turned to face her, speaking with an intensity which startled her companion. "You do not know what it would mean to me to believe that!"

"Of course you may believe it," Dorothy replied reassuringly. She could see that Charmian was deeply agitated, and felt somewhat at a loss, for the conversation had taken a turn she had not expected. So it was with a relief that she saw her brother coming down the steps from the upper terrace, and beckoned imperiously to him to join them.

He came up, doffing his hat and bowing in response to Charmian's somewhat flustered curtsy, and expressed his regret that he had not been at home to greet the visitors when they arrived. Dorothy, ignoring this, said with forced gaiety:

"I have been trying to convince Miss Tarrant, Piers, that we are all going to become very good friends, but I am not sure that she believes me. Come, add your assurances to mine!"

Charmian flushed scarlet with embarrassment, and Piers directed a quelling glance at Dorothy which did not appear to leave her unduly chastened.

"That, surely, is for Miss Tarrant to decide," he said calmly, and turned to Charmian, adding with a smile: "My sister, ma'am, expresses a hope which I share, but she does so, it seems, with more goodwill than delicacy.

You must not feel that you are under any obligation to regard us as your friends."

"The obligation, sir, is wholly mine," she replied in a low voice. "I am already indebted to you for your kindness at our first meeting, for which I fear I did not properly thank you."

She looked up at him as she spoke, and he was struck once again by the sadness in her face. This time, however, he thought to read something else in her eyes—a shadow of fear, a tentative appeal for help? He could not be sure, for their glances met for a moment only, and then her eyes were demurely lowered once more and he could no longer see their expression.

"There is no need to thank me, Miss Tarrant," he said quietly. "It was a privilege to be of service to you, and pray believe that you may command my help at any time, should the need arise."

The words were commonplace enough, yet Charmian felt instinctively that this man said nothing unless he sincerely meant it, and the conviction brought with it a tiny shred of comfort. Dorothy, looking from one to the other, thought the situation decidedly promising, and hastened to take advantage of it.

"I have been thinking, Piers," she informed her brother, "that as this is Miss Tarrant's first visit to Sussex, and I believe Mrs Fenshawe does not care to ride, it would be a good notion for us to show her something of the countryside."

"That would certainly give me great pleasure," he assented at once, "but it must be as Miss Tarrant wishes." He turned to Charmian, adding seriously: "What do you say, ma'am? We know that you are not here on a visit of pleasure, but if it would divert you to explore the countryside hereabouts, I assure you that Dorothy and I will be most happy to be your guides."

"You are very kind, sir, and I would like it exceedingly," Charmian replied eagerly. "I was used to ride a great deal, for I have lived in the country all my life. But I do not know whether it would be considered seemly for me to do so at present."

"We will ask Mama," Dorothy said firmly, "for if *she* says it will be quite proper, Miss Tarrant, you may depend upon it that it is so."

"That is quite true," Piers agreed with a smile. "Will you permit my mother to advise you in this, ma'am? I believe you may do so with complete confidence."

Charmian smiled shyly back at him. She was quite willing to be guided by Lady Wychwood's opinion, for she knew without any doubt at all that if the decision were left to Mrs Fenshawe, the project would be instantly forbidden.

"I am sure I may, Sir Piers," she replied, "and if her ladyship thinks it proper, it will make me very happy to accept so kind an invitation."

"Then let us seek her opinion without delay," he suggested, and offered her his arm. She laid her hand upon it and allowed him to lead her back towards the house, while Dorothy, following them, silently congratulated herself upon the initial success of her first attempt at matchmaking. She had no hesitation in taking upon herself full credit for this very promising beginning.

6

A Spell of Fair Weather

Lady Wychwood, on being appealed to, gave it as her opinion that there was no reason why Miss Tarrant should not go riding with Dorothy and Piers. She called upon Mrs Fenshawe to support her in this, wording the request so skilfully that Lavinia, for all her shrewdness, was unable to disagree, and was obliged to give her consent to a proposal which filled her with vexation and misgiving.

It was arranged that, if the weather continued fine, Dorothy and Piers would come to Bell Orchard the following day, when Charmian would be ready to go with them. Buoyed up by this pleasing prospect, she felt herself able to ignore Lavinia's obvious displeasure, and refused to be dismayed by the ominous silence which Mrs Fenshawe maintained throughout their homeward journey.

Before this was over, an incident occurred to remind her that there were still many matters concerning the Fenshawes of which she knew nothing. They had passed through Wychwood End and reached the crossroads a short way beyond where they must turn sharply along the

road to Bell Orchard. A great tree spread its branches
where the four roads met, and at its foot a woman was
sitting with a baby in her lap. The child had watched with
wondering eyes the approach of the coach and its four
powerful horses, and as it slowed to turn the corner he
shouted with glee and stretched out his little hands, excited by the clatter of hooves and jingle of harness so
close beside him.

With one graceful movement the woman gathered him
in her arms and rose to her feet, and Charmian found herself staring through the window of the coach at the most
beautiful girl she had ever seen. It was a voluptuous, statuesque beauty which might coarsen and fade in later life,
but at present—she was very young—its impact was
startling and enhanced rather than impaired by her plain
country garb of dimity gown and homespun petticoat.
Curls like burnished copper glowed beneath her coarse
straw hat, and though the sturdy boy in her arms had
dark eyes and hair as black as a raven's wing, the likeness
between them was strong enough to mark them unmis-
takably as mother and son.

The girl curtsied respectfully as the coach lumbered by,
but the servility of the gesture was made ridiculous by the
tilt of her head and the mocking insolence in those astonishing, violet-blue eyes as she looked at the two women in
the carriage. When they had passed her, Charmian turned
impulsively to Lavinia to ask who she might be, but was
checked by the sheer fury in the other woman's face. Mrs
Fenshawe was staring straight before her with narrowed
eyes, her lips tightly compressed and a spot of colour
burning in each painted cheek. Charmian had known her
long enough to be able to translate these danger signals,
and to realize that Lavinia's earlier vexation was as nothing to the fury that consumed her now; it would plainly
be wiser to say nothing.

By the following day the incident had faded from her mind, and some time was to pass before she thought of it again. Sir Piers and his sister arrived promptly, and Charmian, who had found herself looking forward to the meeting with an uncommon degree of eagerness, refused to let her pleasure be spoiled by Lavinia's continued ill-humour.

She was a good rider, and found it delightful to be on horseback again, and as her companions knew every inch of the countryside, they led her by pleasant and often unfrequented ways. Crossing the park to the shore, they followed the coast eastwards for several miles until they reached a small fishing village, and there turned inland again along the road which passed the gates of Bell Orchard. The sun shone brightly, its warmth tempered by a fresh breeze from the sea, and Charmian's spirits rose until she felt happier than she had done at any time since her father's death.

In Dorothy's merry company it was impossible to feel depressed. She chattered incessantly, and though for the most part her brother listened with a kind of indulgent resignation, he once or twice intervened to check her bubbling high spirits. Then Dorothy would pout and toss her head, and fall silent for a few minutes, but these exchanges were entirely good-humoured and it was plain that brother and sister were deeply attached to one another. Charmian, watching them, reflected wistfully that Dorothy was much to be envied.

When they reached Bell Orchard again the Wychwoods declined to enter the house. Piers, aiding Miss Tarrant to dismount, thanked her courteously for the pleasure of her company, and Dorothy, still in the saddle, said buoyantly:

"Let us ride again tomorrow! We ought to take advantage of this fine weather while it lasts."

Charmian agreed willingly to this, and then farewells

were said and Piers and Dorothy rode off along the drive. Charmian, entering the house, was met by a servant with the information that Mrs Fenshawe had expressed a desire to speak with her immediately she came in.

Conscious of a feeling of apprehension which she told herself was absurd, she went reluctantly into the front parlour. Lavinia was sitting by the window with a book in her hand, but Charmian felt sure that she had not been reading. The window commanded a view of the entrance drive, and she knew that her hostess must have watched her return with Dorothy and Sir Piers.

"So there you are!" Lavinia greeted her peevishly. "I take it that you enjoyed your ride?"

"Very much, Lavinia, I thank you," Charmian replied equably, and then, since evasion might seem to hint at some disquiet on her own part, she added: "We are to ride again at the same time tomorrow."

"Indeed?" Lavinia laid her book down on the window-seat beside her and spoke deliberately. "If these excursions are to become a daily occurrence, I do not think I can approve of them."

"May I ask why?"

"The reason, surely, is plain enough. You are in mourning."

"If I may go riding one day with perfect propriety, I can see no reason why I should not do so again the next. Lady Wychwood saw no harm in it, and you agreed with her."

Lavinia's lips tightened. "I agreed because in the circumstances I could not do otherwise without discourtesy, but I did not suppose that you intended to make a habit of such jaunts. If you have engaged to ride tomorrow, then you must do so, but that, if you please, will be the end of it."

A sudden anger awoke in Charmian. She might be

afraid of Colonel Fenshawe, but she certainly did not stand in awe of his wife.

"No, Lavinia," she said quietly, "it will not be the end of it. I do not wish to quarrel with you, but you must give me credit for some opinions of my own. For me to ride quietly about the countryside with Miss Wychwood and her brother can outrage nobody, and I feel sure that even Papa himself would not wish me to be denied so harmless a pleasure."

"Very well!" Mrs Fenshawe spoke with a snap. "Since you will not be guided by my advice I will give you the plain facts, and if you find them hurtful you have only yourself to blame. Remember, Charmian, that though to us, who know the whole truth, your father's death was an honourable one, the world at large regards it in a very different light. Suicide is a shocking and disgraceful thing, and the ugly shame of it inevitably clings to the relatives of one who commits it. I do not think the so-correct Sir Piers, or his mother, would condone Dorothy's friendship with you if they were informed of the truth."

Charmian drew a sharp breath and closed her eyes, gripping the back of a chair to steady herself. The unfeeling words brought the manner of her father's death before her again in all its horror, and she knew that, unjust though it was, there would always henceforth be a slight savour of scandal attached to her name. Then she remembered the level directness of Piers Wychwood's eyes, and the wise kindliness in his mother's face, and the memory brought reassurance.

"Do not threaten me, Lavinia," she said, and though her heart thumped painfully her voice was steady enough. "I believe that neither Lady Wychwood nor Sir Piers would think any the worse of me because of something for which I was in no way to blame, and to prove that belief I shall tell them the truth myself. And I shall remain

upon friendly terms with Miss Wychwood as long as she
and they desire it!"

She turned and went out of the room, and as the door
closed behind her Lavinia swore viciously under her
breath. Then, her feelings not wholly relieved by profan-
ity, she snatched up her book and flung it across the
room. She knew that her husband would be displeased
when he learned of Miss Tarrant's growing friendship
with the Wychwoods, but at present she could see no way
to end it. She realized she was handling the affair ineptly,
but between her dislike of life at Bell Orchard, and her
growing uneasiness at the dangerous situation in which
they all found themselves, and in which they would remain until the elusive Rob Dunton could be found, she
was finding it increasingly difficult to remain calm. News
from London was scanty and discouraging, for there was
no sign yet of Dunton walking into the trap which had
been set for him, and neither the Colonel nor Miles could
glean any news of him. From the night of Mr Tarrant's
death, the Jacobite agent had disappeared completely.

The fine weather continued for the rest of that week
and throughout the next, and each day, with the exception
of Sunday, Charmian went riding with her friends from
Wychwood Chase. Mrs Fenshawe's uneasiness was increased by the fact that only twice did Dorothy appear at
Bell Orchard with a middle-aged groom as escort instead
of her brother, and she would have been even more disturbed had she been present during their excursions. As
the days passed, Dorothy, curbing her natural vivacity,
forced herself to take less and less part in the conversation and to assume the rôle of passive and unobtrusive
onlooker. She formed the habit of riding a little way
ahead of her companions, or falling behind them, and
noted with satisfaction that the intervals when they were

unaware of her defection grew longer and more frequent each day.

To Charmian herself it seemed as though she were living in two different worlds, the safe, sane, happy one she shared with Dorothy and Piers, and the other, of taut nerves, secrets and suspicion, which was Bell Orchard. She felt sometimes as though she could endure no longer the tension of life in the old house: Lavinia's petulance, Harry's sullen indifference and flashes of rage, her own ever-present doubts and fears. At such times her one consolation lay in the thought of Piers Wychwood; he was her friend, her only ally; as long as he was within reach, she need not completely despair.

At last, Lavinia's disquiet prompted her to enlist Harry's aid in the matter. She had never been on particularly good terms with her elder stepson, and for more than a year a sort of armed truce had prevailed between them, so that she had been extremely reluctant to ask his help. One day, however, when she had just watched Charmian ride away from the house with Piers and Dorothy, she heard Harry's step in the hall. Jumping up from her chair, she hurried across and flung open the parlour door.

"Harry!" she said sharply. "I wish to speak to you, if you please."

He paused and scowled at her as though half-minded to refuse, then, as she turned back into the room, he came unwillingly to join her. Thrusting the door shut and leaning his shoulders against it, he said ungraciously:

"Well, what is it?"

"Do you need to ask?" Lavinia flung out a hand to point in the direction of the drive. "Did you not see Miss Tarrant ride out with Piers Wychwood and his sister?"

"Of course I saw them," Harry replied irritably, "and a curst long time they took about it. I have been skulking

above-stairs these ten minutes so that you should not have
a brawl on your doorstep. Why the devil do you encourage him to come here so often?"

"I encourage him?" she repeated, outraged. "Upon my
soul, Harry, there are times when your insolence is beyond all bearing! For the past fortnight I have done all in
my power to prevent any sort of intimacy growing up between the Wychwoods and Miss Tarrant."

"Have you, b'Gad?" he retorted mockingly. "Your efforts have not been precisely successful, have they? Why
not just forbid her to go jaunting about the country while
she is in mourning?"

"I have done so," she confessed sulkily, "but she will
pay no heed to me. Then I threatened to tell them that
her father killed himself, and she cut the ground from
beneath my feet by telling them herself. It appears to
have had no effect, though why such a hidebound, nar-
row-minded family should be willing to accept such a
thing I cannot imagine." She paused, and drew a deep
breath, for she hated to admit failure to anyone, and especially to Harry. "I can do no more, since the girl is supposed to be a guest here, and not a prisoner. *You* must
find a way to end her friendship with them."

"I?" He seemed genuinely astonished. "What in hell's
name can I do about it?"

His stepmother glared at him, tapping one foot angrily
upon the floor. "That is for you to decide," she said unpleasantly. "If you had not been so wretchedly stubborn,
you would have the right to forbid her to spend so much
time in their company. I tell you, Harry, it will displease
your father if he discovers that we have allowed
Charmian to be upon such friendly terms with the Wychwoods, when Sir Piers is doing all he can to stir up trouble for us."

"Not for us, m'dear!" For these traitorous Jacobites

who are bribing honest smugglers to ship them across the Channel. Piers would never believe that we have any connexion with that. What, the idle Fenshawes involved in anything as serious as politics? He would find the mere idea absurd."

"How can you be sure of that? How do you know that he is not already suspicious, and hoping that Charmian may betray us? I cannot imagine why else he would be so assiduous in his attentions."

Harry grinned at her, his ill-temper abating as hers increased. "You are growing timid, Lavinia, and your fears blind you to the obvious. What the devil! Piers is flesh-and-blood, is he not, and Miss Tarrant a pretty girl, as well as being an heiress?"

Lavinia frowned. "He cannot know that she is an heiress."

"All London knows it, m'dear, and Lady Wychwood has a sister in town. I'll wager she wrote to Lady Corham as soon as she made Miss Tarrant's acquaintance, and now is doing all in her power to further the affair. Local gossip has it that until two weeks ago Piers was on the point of offering for Selina Grey, and you cannot blame her ladyship for regarding Miss Tarrant as a Heaven-sent alternative."

Mrs Fenshawe appeared to be slightly reassured by this, but said sharply: "Even that is bad enough! I have not endured the company of that tiresome creature all this while in order that her fortune may enrich Piers Wychwood, and I, for one, would not dare to face your father if we permitted such a thing to happen. He would never forgive us!"

"Oh, be easy, m'dear!" Harry was obviously becoming bored with the argument. "Until Miss Tarrant is twenty-one, she cannot marry anyone without the consent of the trustees."

"And do you realize how soon that will be? Besides, there is no reason to suppose that they would refuse their consent if Wychwood asked it. No one can deny that he is extremely eligible." She swung impatiently away and sat down on the window-seat, looking at him with mingled perplexity, and exasperation. "All this would have been avoided if you had done as your father desired. Now I trust you are satisfied with the trouble you have caused!"

A frown darkened Harry's face again, and he said curtly: "I made my intentions plain from the outset, Lavinia, and they are still the same, so you may as well stop plaguing me to marry the confounded girl!"

"But why will you not, in Heaven's name? All we desire is to see Charmian's fortune safely in our pockets. It has not even been suggested that you should give up that low-bred mistress of yours, and I'll warrant she would sooner have you rich than poor! Your marriage to Charmian could make no difference to *her* position."

Harry's face whitened with anger, but he made an unwonted effort to keep his temper under control, and merely said with dangerous quietness:

"I'll have no meddling in my affairs from you, Lavinia! Your time would have been better employed these two years past in persuading Miss Tarrant to look more kindly upon Miles. He is eager enough, both for the girl and her gold!"

"And her preference is very plainly for you—or was, until Piers Wychwood came on the scene." In a sudden, uncontrollable spurt of temper she struck the cushioned seat beside her with her clenched fist. "Oh, was there ever a more exasperating, improvident pair than you and your brother? Between you, you have ruined everything, and God knows where it will all end!"

"Not in my marriage to Charmian Tarrant, I give you my word," Harry informed her shortly, preparing to leave, "and if you will listen to a word of advice, do not make too great an issue of her friendship with the Wychwoods. The association may displease my father, but it will displease him a great deal more if you arouse Piers' suspicions by trying too hard to keep him and Miss Tarrant apart. He is no fool, and he knows as well as we do that there is no reason in the world why they should not be on friendly terms."

"I shall write to your father," Lavinia announced abruptly. "He must decide how to deal with this matter. And," she added spitefully, "I shall tell him how little help you have given me in this difficulty."

"Tell him what you please," Harry said curtly. "*I* was not sent here to keep watch over Miss Tarrant. My task is to deal with Rob Dunton if he comes here, and you may be sure I shall accomplish it more efficiently than you have carried out your part in the affair. What is more, I shall ask no one's help in doing it!"

7

The Cottage by the River

The following day dawned as fine and warm as those which had preceded it, and at the accustomed hour Dorothy and Piers arrived at Bell Orchard. Once again Mrs Fenshawe watched Charmian ride off with them, but this time she was able to console herself with the thought of the letter already despatched to London by the hand of a trusted servant. It would inform Colonel Fenshawe of this unforeseen turn of events, and probably bring him to Sussex to deal with it.

The riders made their way through the park to the coast, intending to ride along the shore as far as the river mouth, and then upstream to the ford and so to Wychwood Chase, where they would take some refreshment before returning to Bell Orchard. Dorothy seemed unusually listless, and once or twice pressed a hand to her forehead as though the glare of the sun on the sea was more than she could bear. At last, with the air of one who, though reluctant to spoil her companions' pleasure, was suffering too much to endure it any longer, she confessed to a severe headache, which had, she said, been troubling her ever since she woke that morning.

The admission was made just as they were passing a farm which stood back from the shore in a fold of the ground, and she followed it up with a suggestion that she should rest there while the others continued their ride. Charmian started to protest, but Piers, looking rather hard at his sister, said dryly:

"That is an excellent notion! Mrs Channock will look after you, and I can come back to the farm when I have escorted Miss Tarrant home." He saw Charmian's doubtful expression and smiled faintly. "Do not look so disturbed, ma'am. The situation, I believe, is one in which convention may be set aside a trifle."

She was not entirely convinced, but since Dorothy was plainly far from being her usual sprightly self, she felt that it would be unkind to raise any objection. So Miss Wychwood was duly escorted to the farm and handed over to the care of its kindly and much concerned mistress, and Charmian, having seen her comfortably settled in the parlour, went, still with some reluctance, to rejoin Piers. They crossed the fields again to the shore, riding in silence until Charmian said diffidently:

"I think, sir, that it will be best if I do not come to Wychwood Chase today. It is certain to cause Lady Wychwood concern when she learns of your sister's indisposition, and besides, it would be unkind to leave Miss Wychwood alone at the farm for so long."

"Perhaps you are right, Miss Tarrant," he agreed pleasantly. "We will cut back through the woods, then, to Bell Orchard, though I hope that we may have the pleasure of entertaining you at the Chase in the near future."

She thanked him, and assured him rather shyly that she shared that hope, and they rode on along the sunlit shore

until they reached the outskirts of the cluster of fisher-
men's cottages about the river mouth. Skirting the edge of
the hamlet, they turned inland along a track which followed the winding course of the lazy stream. The sand-
dunes gave place to rough pasture where sheep grazed,
and then to more fertile meadows, and at length they
passed into the welcome shade of the woods.

Piers had been chatting pleasantly as they rode, but
though Charmian responded to his remarks, her thoughts
were not wholly upon them. In spite of her defiant words
to Lavinia nearly a fortnight before, she had never spoken
to the Wychwoods of her father's death, for a suitable opportunity to do so had never seemed to present itself, and
she had been secretly glad of the fact. Now, however, that
excuse for what she knew to be cowardice was no longer
valid, and she was trying to nerve herself to broach the
subject. They were well into the woods before she finally
summoned up sufficient courage, but at length, with a
kind of desperation, she said jerkily:

"Sir Piers, there is something I have to tell you, something which it is only right that you should know. It
concerns my father."

She paused, shrinking even now from putting into
words the thing which still had the power to leave her
sick and shaken whenever she thought of it, and Piers regarded her compassionately. He had known from the first
that some trouble weighed heavily upon her, something
other than her natural grief for her father, and he had
hoped that in time she might bring herself to confide in
him. That was why he had agreed so readily to leaving
Dorothy at the farm, even though he felt some doubt as
to the reality of her indisposition.

Charmian was staring straight ahead, her face white
and strained as she tried to find the courage to continue.

Piers leaned across to grasp her horse's bridle, bringing both animals to a halt.

"Miss Tarrant," he said quietly, "if you are about to tell me of the manner of your father's death, I beg that you will not harrow your feelings by speaking of it. I am aware of the circumstances."

"You know?" Charmian's head jerked back towards him; her eyes were wide and startled. "But how?"

"From my aunt, Lady Corham, in London. She and my mother correspond frequently." He paused, gravely studying her troubled face, and then added gently: "It makes no difference, you know!"

Charmian's lips trembled. "It caused a great scandal," she said unsteadily. "I do not think it will ever be quite forgotten."

"Idle tongues can be cruel," Piers agreed slowly, "and malice makes sorrow doubly hard to bear. Try to believe, though, that there are those who wish to be truly your friends."

"I do believe it, sir," she replied softly. "You have made it possible for me to do so."

"I am glad of that," he said seriously, "for I would not wish there to be any misunderstanding between us."

A little silence fell, broken only by the sleepy gurgle of the river, and the jingle of harness as one of the horses tossed its head. Charmian hovered on the brink of further confidences, of disclosing to Piers the secret of Bell Orchard and her own uncertainties and fears, but still conflicting feelings held her back. Would she be able to convince him? Colonel Fenshawe was too clever to let any whisper of his activities leak out, for their success depended upon his remaining above suspicion. She had only her word to offer, and Piers might not accept that against a family whom, however little he might like them, he had known all his life.

His gaze was still fixed upon her face, and the blue-grey eyes held a warmth which set her heart beating faster, and made Jacobite conspiracies seem suddenly distant and unimportant. In breathless confusion she looked away, past him to the river sparkling a dozen yards beyond. Then a movement at the water's edge caught her attention; she looked more directly towards it, her heart gave a lurch of alarm, and she was obliged to stifle a dismayed exclamation. On the very brink of the river, so absorbed that he was unaware of the riders, was a tiny boy, a black-haired baby in a homespun smock. Squatting on his heels, he was beating at the water with a long twig, obviously delighted by the splashes and innocent of his danger.

Piers turned in the saddle, his glance following the direction of her pointing hand, and then without a word he dismounted and handed his horse's rein to her. She watched, holding her breath, as he went slowly and carefully towards the river bank, for she knew that any sudden sound might startle the child and send him tumbling headlong into the water. An eternity seemed to pass before Piers reached him and bent to sweep him swiftly and surely out of danger.

He came quickly back to the path with his prize now kicking and screaming with fright, and Charmian dropped the reins of both horses and stretched out her hands, saying impetuously:

"Oh, poor mite! Give him to me, Sir Piers!"

He obeyed with considerable relief and she clasped the struggling infant in her arms, holding him close and soothing him until his yells subsided into sobs. Then, looking again at Piers, she said indignantly:

"What can his mother be thinking of, to let him wander into such danger? Do you know who he is, sir?"

There was a hesitation, so slight as to be almost imperceptible, before he replied.

"It is Amy Godsall's son," he said briefly.

"Godsall?" Charmian knitted her brows. "Martha Godsall is housekeeper at Bell Orchard."

Piers nodded. "Yes, I know. The family has served the Fenshawes for generations. Jack Godsall, who is Martha's brother and father to Amy, is keeper on the estate. His cottage is a little farther on, a short way back from the river. The boy must have strayed from there."

Charmian looked down at the baby in her arms. He had stopped crying and was staring up curiously into her face, a remarkably handsome child in spite of the dirt and tears staining his small countenance. As she wiped them away with her handkerchief, there came into her mind a picture of the beautiful girl who had curtsied so mockingly as the Fenshawe coach went by, a girl who had held this sturdy lad in her arms.

"We must take him home at once," she said. "If he has been missed, his mother must be half-crazed with anxiety."

Again Piers hesitated, and she had the impression that he was seeking some alternative course. None offered, and with a slight shrug he swung into the saddle again and they went on their way.

A short distance farther on a path branched away to the right, climbing a gentle slope, and as Piers led the way along it they heard a woman's voice calling anxiously somewhere ahead of them. Then they emerged from beneath the trees into brilliant sunshine, and Charmian found herself looking across a clearing at a cottage, an ancient building with thick walls veined with massive beams, and tiny windows which peered like knowing eyes from beneath shaggy thatch.

It should have been a pleasant place, a picturesque

homestead set in the heart of the summer woods, and yet there hung about it an indescribable aura of evil. Even on that bright morning it seemed to exude darkness, as though the ancient walls had looked upon black deeds, and knew secrets which could not be whispered even in the dead of night. Charmian felt her skin prickle with primitive, unreasoning dread, and her clasp on the child tightened so that he gave a protesting cry.

An aged crone who was crouched, wringing her hands, on the bench by the cottage door, looked up sharply, revealing a wrinkled, vulturine face, and on the far side of the clearing, where she had been searching frantically in the undergrowth, Amy Godsall spun round towards the newcomers. For an instant she stared, her eyes enormous in her pallid face, and then, with a cry, came flying across the little garden to snatch her baby from Charmian's arms and strain him to her breast in an agony of relief.

"You should keep a closer watch upon the boy, Amy," Piers said sternly. "Had Miss Tarrant not caught sight of him down by the river, he might well have drowned."

Amy looked quickly up at him and then at Charmian, who was struck afresh by her extraordinary beauty. She said in a low, passionate voice:

"Then God bless 'ee, miss, for 'twould break my heart if any harm came to him. I left him wi' Granny yonder and she fell asleep in the sun, being old and weary like. It be main hard keeping watch on him, he be that venturesome."

"I am sure it must be," Charmian replied gently, "and I am thankful that we found him in time."

She broke off as a man came quickly round the corner of the cottage, a tall man, hatless and coatless, his shirt open at the throat. He stopped short at sight of the newcomers, but Amy turned eagerly towards him.

"Our boy be safe, Harry!" she exclaimed joyfully. "Sir

Piers and the young lady brought him home. They found him down by the river."

"Did they, b'Gad!" Harry Fenshawe strolled forward, apparently in no way abashed by the situation. "Then we are devilish grateful to them."

"Come, Miss Tarrant," Piers said quietly. "There is no need for us to linger here."

"One moment!" Harry laid his hand on the bridle of Charmian's horse; his voice was mocking. "Amy, take the boy indoors!"

She hesitated, looking quickly from one to the other, and then turned and went into the cottage. The old woman got up from the bench and hobbled after her.

"So Sir Piers and the young lady brought the little devil safely home," Harry said softly. "And why, may I ask, are Sir Piers and the young lady riding through the woods alone? Dorothy must be a most accommodating chaperone!"

"Neither matter is any concern of yours!" Piers was making a praiseworthy effort to hide his anger, but his voice had lost some of its normal calm. "Be good enough to stand aside."

"It is very much my concern," Harry retorted with a grin. "Miss Tarrant is in my stepmother's care, so I stand now in much the same position as you did when you objected so strongly to me riding with your sister. You, my friend, should practise what you preach!"

"If that is meant for a jest," Piers said contemptuously, "it is in very poor taste, but I will give you credit for not intending it seriously."

"Obliging of you!" Harry replied derisively. "Of course, Piers Wychwood is to be trusted, and that rake, Harry Fenshawe, is not! Well, perhaps that is true, though devil knows you used not to be so curst righteous!" He released Charmian's horse and stepped back, indicating the path out of the clearing with an airy flourish of his hand. "Ride on, Miss Tarrant! I am persuaded that neither your reputation nor your virtue is in danger."

She was glad enough to escape, and spurred past him with colour blazing hotly in her cheeks. As she rode down the slope towards the river she heard Harry's mocking laughter pursuing her, and urged her mount to a swifter pace. After a moment Piers drew alongside her and said abruptly:

"I must ask your pardon for that incident, Miss Tarrant. Had I known that Harry was at the cottage, nothing would have persuaded me to take you there."

"It is of no importance," she replied, not looking at him. "The child had to be returned to his mother." She paused, and then added irrelevantly: "She is very beautiful."

"Too beautiful for her own good," Piers replied quietly. "One should not blame her too greatly, I suppose, for her mother died when she was born, and her father is a harsh, overbearing fellow. He kept her almost a prisoner in that cottage, and would let no man come near her."

Charmian turned her head to look at him with a puzzled frown, embarrassment overcome by curiosity. "But Mr Fenshawe—" she said doubtfully.

Piers shrugged. "Jack Godsall is dependent upon Colonel Fenshawe for his home and his livelihood," he replied dryly. "He could not send the Colonel's son about his business as he had sent the village lads. To give Harry his due, I believe that he is sincerely attached to Amy, and it is certain that since he took her under his protection, her father has been obliged to treat her less harshly."

He paused, regarding Charmian with some concern, for she was very pale now. He attributed this to the shock of what she had just discovered, and reproached himself for allowing her to dwell upon it.

"I am a thoughtless fool!" he said abruptly. "This matter has distressed you."

"No!" Charmian turned quickly to look at him. It seemed of immense importance for him to understand that Harry Fenshawe did not matter to her in the least. "That does not concern me at all. It was that place, that cottage! You may think this absurd, but to me it seemed to reek of evil."

Piers gave her a curious look. "I wonder why you should think that?" he said musingly. "Have you, perhaps, been listening to the tales the villagers tell concerning old Granny Godsall?" The bewilderment in her face answered him, and he shook his head. "No, I see that you have not! They say, Miss Tarrant, that she is a witch."

"A witch?" Charmian shivered, remembering the old woman at the cottage, her face with its beak-like nose and wrinkled, parchment-coloured skin, the eyes bright and hooded as a snake's. "She has the look of one!"

"The looks and the reputation," Piers replied calmly. "The one built largely upon the other. No, that is not entirely true! She certainly has an extraordinary knowledge of herbs and their uses—my father was used to say that Granny Godsall knew more of such matters than many an apothecary—and the country folk go to her for cures for all ailments, both for themselves and for their animals. I know that she transacts such business with all the trappings of black magic, and I suspect that she is not averse to adding to her profits in less innocent ways. A love-philtre or a waxen image of an enemy must command a far higher price than a mere draught of medicine. It is not surprising that she is thought to possess the evil eye."

"Perhaps she does," Charmian said in a low voice.

"That place breathes the very spirit of terror and despair."

Piers laughed. "Miss Tarrant," he said firmly, "I shall not permit you to indulge in so morbid a fancy! The cottage is very old, and doubtless there are dark pages in its history as there must be in the history of any ancient building, but I assure you that there is no witchcraft there."

She smiled, knowing that he was right, that such superstitions were for credulous country folk, to be mocked at by people of education. Yet she could not cast off the impression the cottage had made upon her; even to think of it brought a cold feeling of dread, and she hoped fervently that she need never see the place again.

The feeling continued to haunt her even after her return to Bell Orchard. Piers took his leave and rode away, having promised, in answer to her anxious insistence, to keep her informed of the state of his sister's health, and Charmian went up to her bedchamber to change from her riding-habit into a gown. The events of the morning had given her a good deal to think about, and when she had changed she sat down on the window-seat, feeling disinclined for Lavinia's company.

Amy Godsall's defiant attitude was now explained, and so was the insolent familiarity with which the housekeeper, Martha Godsall, occasionally treated her mistress. It was small wonder that Lavinia, with her exaggerated sense of her own importance, found the situation infuriating.

Charmian recalled Mrs Fenshawe's broad hints of hopes for a marriage between Harry and herself, and wondered whether Amy was the reason for his refusal to consider it. It did not seem likely. A man might keep a mistress, and even be deeply devoted to her, but he did not on that account refuse to marry a wealthy woman of his own class. Such marriages were usually matters of arrangement, and a wife was expected to turn a blind eye to her husband's other attachments.

She sighed, and got up again to study her reflection in the mirror. She knew that she was accounted a pretty girl, but the face that looked back at her now seemed plain and commonplace. Black did not become her; it made her look too pale, and brown hair and eyes were not flattered by it; one needed Lavinia's cool, blonde colouring, or the red-gold hair of the girl at the cottage, to wear it to advantage; and it would be a year before she was able to appear in colours again. She unpinned the veil of fine black crêpe which fell from the top of her head to behind her shoulders, and replaced it with a little cap of lace and ribbon, but could not feel that she had profited much by the change.

She did not see Harry again until that evening, when he returned to Bell Orchard, but then it happened that she was descending the stairs just as he entered the house. She halted near the foot of the staircase, conscious of considerable embarrassment, but Harry was apparently immune to such feelings. Tossing his hat, gloves and whip on to the table, he came straight across the hall towards her.

"Miss Tarrant," he said abruptly in a low voice, "it occurs to me that I did not properly thank you for bringing the child safely home. Believe me, I am deeply grateful!"

Surprise for a moment or two deprived her of speech. Harry, looking up at her as she stood above him on the stairs, added almost apologetically:

"The truth is, ma'am, that I am devilish fond of the brat."

"That is natural, sir," she stammered, feeling quite at a loss. "He—he seems an engaging child."

"He is a mischievous little devil," he replied flatly, "but

for all that, I would not wish any harm to come to him. I must ask your pardon, too, for the way I spoke to you. It was outrageous!"

Surprise was crowding upon surprise. Charmian said faintly: "It is forgotten, sir! I know it must have looked odd to you, but Miss Wychwood became indisposed—"

"Lord, m'dear, you have no need to explain to me," he said hastily, "nor to Lavinia, either, for I swear I'll not blab! Piers is the best of good fellows, and we were good friends until he grew so curst sober, but now I cannot resist picking a quarrel with him whenever we meet. For all that, I know I could trust him if the need arose."

It seemed an odd thing to say, even though it confirmed her own opinion of Piers Wychwood, and for one crazy moment she wondered if Harry were showing her a way out of her dilemma, telling her where she might safely seek the help she so sorely needed. The briefest reflection, however, convinced her that she must be mistaken. He would be as concerned as the rest of his family to prevent the secret of their conspiracies from being betrayed, and she was reading a significance which was not intended into words meant to be taken at face value.

Somewhere above them a door opened, and Lavinia's voice was heard issuing some instruction to her maid. A faint frown crossed Harry's face, and he stepped aside so that Charmian might pass him, and then went briskly up the stairs. She heard him exchange a curt word of greeting with his stepmother, and then, as Lavinia's footsteps approached, she sped quickly across the hall and into the parlour. From every point of view, it would be best if Mrs Fenshawe remained in ignorance of the events of the day.

8

Contraband

Charmian had determined that, if no news of Dorothy reached her by the time they usually met, she would go to Wychwood Chase to inquire after her, but during the evening, clouds began to pile up in the west, and she awoke next morning to the sound of rain beating against her window.

The downpour continued throughout the morning with a steady, relentless determination which made any outdoor activity impossible. It veiled the distances in a grey mist, dripped monotonously from the eaves, and trickled in rivulets down the garden paths. The sky was leaden, seeming to rob everything of colour and making the low-pitched, panelled rooms at Bell Orchard so dark that the ladies were obliged to call for candles before they could read or sew.

The gloom out-of-doors had its effect upon tempers within. Lavinia, whose dislike of her country home in fine weather was negligible compared to her loathing of it when the weather was bad, complained bitterly and unceasingly of the circumstances which obliged her to remain there. Charmian felt acutely uncomfortable: she was as weary of Lavinia's company as Lavinia was of hers, but for the sake of good manners had hitherto striven to maintain some show of cordiality. This would never again be possible.

Midway through the afternoon the rain ceased, and though the grey, lowering sky suggested that the respite would be of short duration, she decided to take advantage of it and go for a walk. Lavinia's peevishness had frayed her own temper, and the gloom and heaviness of the day induced a curious sense of being imprisoned, so that she felt she could not bear to be confined any longer to the house. Donning her stoutest shoes and a hooded cloak of fine cloth, she went out into the dripping gardens.

Passing through them, she set out across the park along the route which she and Dorothy and Piers had followed the previous day, for she was conscious of a desire for the open shore and the vast, empty expanse of the sea. Only there, she felt, would she be free of this illogical feeling of confinement, of being caught in a trap from which there was no escape. The rain-sodden grass soaked her shoes and the bottom of her skirts, and as she passed beneath the trees, heavy drops of water dripped from their branches on to her head and shoulders, but there was a freshness in the air which was very pleasant, and slowly her taut nerves relaxed and she was able to put Bell Orchard and its inhabitants from her mind for a time.

She reached the shore at last, and stood for a while watching the grey waves breaking on the grey pebbles, for it was close upon high tide. Then she turned and walked slowly along the beach, still following, almost unconsciously, the path they had ridden the day before, while her thoughts, no longer troubled, drifted pleasantly, soothed by the rhythmic voice of the sea.

It began to rain again, not heavily as before, but softly,

almost caressingly, and with a sigh of regret she turned
once more towards Bell Orchard. This time she followed
a different path, crossing a stretch of rough grassland to
the belt of trees which at that point bordered the park.
Beyond the trees was a lane leading to the home farm and
the stable-yard, and a short way along it stood a barn, a
roomy, stonebuilt place with a steeply sloping roof.

The rain was falling faster now, and it occurred to her
that it might be wiser to avail herself of the shelter close
at hand than to continue on her way. She hastened her
steps, and was fairly within the barn before she realized
that it was already occupied. A cart stood there, with a
patient horse between the shafts, and in one corner of the
barn a heap of straw had been dragged aside to reveal a
pile of small wooden kegs, which two brawny countrymen
were engaged in transferring to the cart. It seemed so
curious an occupation that at first perplexity was her only
reaction. She stood and stared, until one of the men
turned his head and saw her.

He voiced a curse and heaved the keg he was holding
swiftly into the cart, while his companion swung round to
learn the cause of his dismay. Then, in unspoken agreement which was in itself disquieting, both advanced
towards her. She fell back a pace, bewilderment giving
way to alarm, but the taller of the two was already between her and the doorway, stretching out an arm to
block her path.

"Spy on us, would 'ee?" he said roughly. "Come creep-
ing to pry into matters as don't concern 'ee?"

"No, no!" she faltered, still completely at a loss. "I
only wished to shelter from the rain."

The other man laughed harshly. "A likely tale!" he
jeered. "We've a short way wi' spies, my lass! One as will
teach 'ee a lesson ye'll not forget."

She shrank back, not comprehending how she had offended, but sharply aware of her danger in that lonely spot. Then, with a relief so great that for an instant she wondered whether her senses had deceived her, she caught the sound of approaching hoofbeats. Harry, perhaps, returning from Godsall's cottage.

With a suddenness which took the two men unawares, she ducked beneath the outstretched arm and darted out into the lane, hearing them curse as they pounded in pursuit. Panic lent her speed as she fled towards the approaching horseman, still hidden from view by a bend in the lane, and then she slipped on the wet ground and fell headlong, knocking all the breath from her body.

Strong hands seized her by the arms and hauled her to her feet as the rider, rounding the bend, saw the little group before him and spurred his mount forward. He came to a plunging halt beside them and his whip cracked resoundingly across the shoulders of the nearer man, making him swear and release his hold on Charmian.

"What the devil—?" It was Piers' voice, taut with anger. "Stand back, the pair of you! Have you taken leave of your senses?"

As the two hurriedly obeyed him, he sprang from the saddle and stepped quickly to Charmian's side. She was still breathless with fright and the shock of the fall, and clung thankfully to his arm.

"My dear Miss Tarrant!" Piers' voice was full of urgent concern. "Have these two ruffians harmed you?"

She shook her head. "They were in the barn," she faltered. "I went to shelter from the rain and—and they threatened me!"

One of the men sullenly muttered something about strangers and spies, and Piers said sharply:

"You confounded fool, the lady comes from Bell Orchard! I imagine that Colonel Fenshawe will have a word to say when he learns it is no longer safe for his guests to walk abroad on his estate." Ignoring their sheepish protests, he looked again at Charmian. "Miss Tarrant, you have been badly frightened. Let us step into the barn, where you may sit down for a few minutes, and when you have recovered a little I will take you home."

She obeyed without protest, leaning gratefully on his arm, for it was now raining heavily once more. Within the barn Piers paid no heed, beyond a single, comprehending glance, to the cart and its mysterious load but found a seat for Charmian on a pile of hurdles, saying curtly over his shoulder to the two men who were now hovering uneasily in the doorway:

"Fetch my horse, one of you, and then take your wagon and go. And think yourselves lucky to escape so easily!"

They hastened to do his bidding, the younger one hurrying to lead in the horse while the elder heaved the few remaining kegs into the cart with the utmost dispatch. Straw was hastily tossed over them, one of the men went to the horse's head, and the cart lumbered forward out of the barn into the slanting spears of rain.

Piers, who had watched these activities with an air of controlled impatience, turned back to Charmian. She was calmer now, and able to feel conscious of her bedraggled appearance, her cloak and gown plastered with mud, her hair falling in damp, dishevelled curls about her face. She had grazed her right hand badly when she fell, and had been trying, without much success, to bandage it with a wisp of handkerchief already stained with mud and blood.

Piers sat down beside her and, taking her hand gently in his, proceeded to bind it with his own larger handkerchief, paying no heed to her faint protest. For a moment or two she was silent, studying his down-bent fair head and serious face, and then she said in a puzzled voice:

"I do not understand! Why were they so angry that I had seen them here?"

"Why?" He glanced up, smiling faintly, before returning to his task. "Because, Miss Tarrant, you are a stranger to them, and had caught them in the act of shifting contraband goods."

"Contraband?" she repeated in a stunned voice. "You mean those men are smugglers?"

"Certainly, when they are not being honest labourers." Piers knotted the handkerchief and looked up, a gleam of amusement in his eyes. "But then we are all smugglers here, to a greater or lesser degree."

She stared at him, torn between disbelief and shock, and the amusement in his eyes deepened to a smile.

"I am not jesting, ma'am. Oh, I do not mean that we all go down to the beach on moonless nights and haul the cargo ashore—though I have done that before now." He paused to laugh ruefully at the recollection. "When Harry Fenshawe and I were boys, we counted it a great adventure if we could take a hand in running a cargo. We did so, too, on several occasions, until our respective fathers learned of it. That put an end to active smuggling—for me, at all events, though it would not surprise me to learn that Harry still helps with a run from time to time. He has the nature for it, and Jack Godsall is the leader of all the smugglers hereabouts."

"But surely," Charmian protested in bewilderment, "it cannot be done as openly as this? Do the authorities take no measures to prevent it?"

Piers shrugged. "The Excisemen should do so, of course, but, in this neighbourhood at least, they seem extraordinarily unwilling to take any action. That casts the whole responsibility upon the magistrates, such as myself, who are also landowners. Nine out of ten of our labourers and tenants have a hand in the smuggling trade, and we could not turn them all over to the law. Nor would we, even if we could. It has been going on for generations and, as I say, we are all smugglers along the Sussex coast. It is exceedingly reprehensible, no doubt, but I am obliged to own that most of the brandy in my cellars, and many of the silks and laces my mother and sister wear, never had a penny of duty paid on them. And I have no doubt at all that the same is true at Bell Orchard."

Charmian was silent, trying to adjust her mind to this new and startling outlook. Hitherto she had thought of smuggling, if she thought of it at all, as a furtive and dangerous practice carried on in secret at dead of night, but here it seemed to be an accepted, almost respectable occupation, inextricably mingled with the commonplace tasks of every day.

"Even the clergy turn a blind eye to it, Miss Tarrant," Piers said quietly, as though guessing the trend of her thoughts. "I have known times when the church bells could not be rung because of the quantity of contraband hidden in the tower, and there is more than one tomb from which spirits of a very tangible kind issue in the dark of the moon."

"What would have happened to me, sir, if you had not come when you did?"

Piers frowned. "You might have been handled somewhat roughly, even made prisoner for a time, but they would have let you go as soon as they realized who you are. I will see to it that word of what happened reaches Jack Godsall, and he will make sure that nothing of the kind occurs again. My assurance to those fellows may not be sufficient, for at present I am regarded with suspicion. The rumour has spread that I am seeking to put a stop to all smuggling in these parts."

Charmian, now completely out of her depth, asked faintly: "And are you, Sir Piers?"

He laughed. "I know better than to attempt the impossible, ma'am. No, all I am trying to do is to end a more dangerous traffic in which Godsall has lately been indulging—the smuggling into England of Jacobite agents along with his silks and brandy."

Charmian's heart gave a great lurch, and began to pound so violently that it seemed her companion must surely hear it. In a voice she scarcely recognized as her own she heard herself ask: "Are you sure?"

"*I* am sure, ma'am, but I am finding it exceedingly hard to convince anyone else of it," he replied ruefully. "You see, I have no proof, and without it, no one is inclined to take me seriously. All I have to go upon myself is the word of a dead man."

"A dead man?" she repeated. "I do not understand."

"One night last spring, Miss Tarrant," he explained, "there was an extremely bad storm, and the next morning, as I rode along the shore, I came upon a man lying at the water's edge. The poor fellow must have been swept overboard from some ship, probably a smuggling craft, and though he had succeeded in reaching land, the struggle, and the subsequent exposure to the cold as he lay exhausted upon the beach, had proved too much for him. I did what I could, but it was plain that he was at the point of death, only partly conscious and unaware of my presence. He seemed greatly troubled, and from his disjointed mutterings I gathered that he was a Jacobite messenger, the bearer of important letters from the Pretender to his supporters in England, but even in his extremity he named no names. He died before I could summon help."

"But you spoke of letters," she protested. "Did they not provide the proof you needed?"

"Ah, the letters!" he said with a rueful laugh. "They were clutched in his hand, and close by lay the piece of oiled silk in which they had been wrapped for protection. His last thought had been to prevent them from falling into unfriendly hands, and he had torn them into fragments and thrust them into the wet sand. Not a word was decipherable."

"And no one believed you when you told them what you knew?"

He shrugged. "They listened courteously enough, and promised to look into the matter, but that was the end of it. I even carried my tale to London, and fared no better there than here."

Charmian was silent for a moment or two, and then she said diffidently: "If this unfortunate man had been swept overboard and swam ashore, he might have no connection with this part at all. Help might have been waiting for him in quite another place."

Piers shook his head. "I think not, ma'am! Even before that day I had heard rumours of mysterious strangers whom Godsall had brought ashore from time to time, but I had paid little heed to them. Now, of course, I hear nothing, and if any Jacobites have come ashore, they have been whisked very speedily out of sight, though by what means I cannot imagine. Godsall, I am sure, has no political convictions. His only concern is money."

There was another pause, while Charmian wrestled with the problem of whether or not to tell him that it was at Bell Orchard that the Jacobites found support and shelter. Such an opporunity to speak might never occur again, but still she was conscious of doubt, reluctance to set in motion something which she would be powerless to halt.

"Sir Piers," she said timidly at length, "even if what you suspect is true, is there any real danger from it? I know little of politics, but I cannot see what can be achieved by these secret comings and goings."

"I am no politician, Miss Tarrant," he replied gravely. "My interests lie in the handling of my estate and in discharging my duties as squire as best I may. I have no way of knowing how strong or how weak is the party in England which supports the Stuarts. Most Jacobites here, I believe, are content merely to talk, to drink the health of the King 'over the water' and damnation to King George, but there are two facts which cannot be ignored. Charles Edward Stuart is in France, and is almost certain to make an attempt to recover the English throne, as his father did thirty years ago. Such an attempt can only be made by force of arms, and even if it fails, as I think it must, there is bound to be bloodshed."

Charmian looked out through the open doorway of the barn at the green countryside, misted with falling rain. It was difficult to connect that gentle prospect with thoughts of battle and armed rebellion.

"Bloodshed?" she repeated. "Here?"

"Perhaps," Piers said quietly. "When the Pretender strikes I think he will do so in Scotland, as his father did, for the Highland clans are his most loyal adherents, but if he comes with French aid, the Jacobites in England and Wales may rise also. Remember that the greater part of our army is still in Flanders." He rose to his feet and walked across to the door and stood looking out. "Civil war, Miss Tarrant! Englishmen fighting their friends and kinsmen, as they did a century ago! That is what I think of, the suffering of ordinary folk, rather than of the rights of kings and princes. That is what I would do anything in my power to avert."

There was silence for a space, broken only by the patter of the raindrops and the restless movements of the horse tethered in the far corner of the barn. Charmian's thoughts spun anxiously, as she considered Piers' words, and remembered her father, who had poured his whole fortune into the Stuart cause, and for what? That men might fight and die, and their womenfolk be left, lonely and bereaved, to weep for them as she had wept for him? She looked across at Piers, glad now of the circumstances which had given them this chance to talk, and grateful that he had unwittingly resolved her doubts and fears. She must tell him what she knew; it was her clear duty.

"Sir Piers," she said abruptly, before her resolution had time to fade, "you say you are puzzled to know what becomes of these men whom the smugglers bring ashore. Suppose they were guided to a house where they could be sure of aid and protection, and of being provided with the means to continue their journey?" She hesitated for just one moment longer, and then took the step which could never be retraced. "To Bell Orchard, for instance."

At her first words he had turned to face her, but with all the light behind him, she could not see his expression. She expected some positive reaction to her words, astonishment, incredulity, perhaps even anger at such an accusation, but none of these came. Piers shook his head, and when he spoke, his voice was calm and even faintly amused.

"A plausible theory, Miss Tarrant, and one which had already occurred to me—if there were any house near here which might fill the part you suggest. Bell Orchard certainly does not."

"How can you say so? It stands alone and close to the shore, so that there are a dozen ways in which one may approach unobserved from the sea. You say the man Godsall is the leader of the smugglers, and he is employed by Colonel Fenshawe—"

"My dear Miss Tarrant, all this is undoubtedly true, but there is one thing you have forgotten, which makes nonsense of all the rest." Piers came back and stood looking down at her, and now she could see that he was smiling. "Colonel Fenshawe is not a Jacobite!"

"How do you know, sir, that he is not?"

"Because I have known him all my life!" Piers set one foot on the pile of hurdles and leaned his elbow on his knee, regarding her with a quizzical smile. "I fear, ma'am, that my disclosure to you of our smuggling activities has led you to believe us capable of all manner of villainy. The Colonel takes no active part in politics, but I have not the smallest doubt that he is loyal to the established Government, if only because he is too practical a man to lend himself to a cause so nearly lost as that of the Stuart kings. As for Harry and Miles, the one is concerned only with amusing himself, while the other devotes so much thought to the set of his wig and the cut of his coat that he has no room in his mind for anything else. No, one might as well look for Jacobites at Wychwood Chase as at Bell Orchard."

She made no reply, but sat with bent head, tracing a pattern on the dusty floor with the toe of her shoe. This was the one thing for which she had not been prepared, this refusal to take her accusation seriously. Yet how could she expect to convince him? She had no proof to offer. There had been nothing among her father's effects to betray his allegiance to the exiled King, and as for Colonel Fenshawe, she could only repeat what he had told her before returning to London, setting her word against his and knowing that he would deny it and probably give convincing proof of his loyalty to King George.

She realized suddenly that there was a grim irony in the situation. No one would listen to Piers' warnings concerning the Jacobites, and now he was refusing to believe that she could provide him with the proof he sought. She could think of no way of convincing him, and he, supposing from her silence that the subject held no further interest for her, said with a smile:

"Do you know, Miss Tarrant, that the circumstances of our meeting had driven out of my mind the reason for my presence here? When I came upon you just now I was on my way to Bell Orchard to bring you a message from my sister."

"Oh!" Charmian exclaimed guiltily, for until that moment she had forgotten her earlier anxiety concerning Dorothy. "How is she, sir? I should have inquired sooner after her health!"

"She finds herself completely recovered, ma'am," he replied, in a dry tone which puzzled her a little, "but my mother considered it unwise for her to venture out in such inclement weather. So I undertook to carry her apologies to you, after I had dealt with some business at the cottages by the river mouth."

"That was kind of you, Sir Piers! I meant to ride over to see how she did, but the rain prevented it. I am so glad that she is better." She looked up at him and smiled. "I must count myself fortunate, too, that you happened to come by when you did, for I do not think I could have convinced those men that I meant them no harm, and in fact did not even realize what they were about."

He laughed. "They would find that hard to believe, I admit. As I said, smuggling is a tradition along the Sussex coast." He glanced over his shoulder, and then took his foot from the hurdles and stood erect. "I believe the rain is stopping. I had better take you home before Mrs Fenshawe grows anxious."

Charmian stifled a sigh and got up, smoothing down her creased and muddied skirts, while Piers went to untether his horse. Leading the animal into the middle of the barn, he said:

"Will you finish the journey mounted, Miss Tarrant?

You will find it more comfortable, I think, than walking through the mire."

She assented, and allowed him to lift her on to the horse's back, and he led the animal out of the barn and along the lane towards Bell Orchard. Charmian was silent, thinking of her dishevelled appearance and the caustic comments it would provoke from Lavinia, even if she returned to the house as she had left it, alone and on foot. To arrive there escorted by Piers Wychwood, and mounted on his horse, while Lavinia was in her present mood, would precipitate a scene from the mere prospect of which she shrank in dismay.

Just before the buildings of farm and stables came in sight, a path branched off from the lane to serve a gate in the wall of the rose-garden, a short distance away to the right. Charmian leaned forward.

"Will you think me very ungrateful, sir, if I suggest that we part here?" she said anxiously. "Mrs Fenshawe may consider it a trifle odd if you escort me to the house."

He halted and turned to look at her, and she saw comprehension in his eyes. He nodded.

"I understand, Miss Tarrant, and the last thing I desire is to cause you embarrassment. We will part here, if that is what you wish. No misadventure, I think, can befall you between here and the house."

"Yes, this is the second time you have found me in need of rescue," she said as he came to help her to the ground. "What a tiresome creature you must think me! You will grow weary, sir, of coming to my assistance."

He lifted her down and stood for a moment, holding her lightly by the arms and studying her face with an expression which brought the colour stealing into her cheeks.

"That I could never do," he said seriously. "I have always wanted to help you, from the very first moment I saw you. Do you know when that was? The last time I was in London I chanced to pass Colonel Fenshawe's house late one night, and you came out with an old gentleman. You wore a ballgown and jewels and powdered hair, but your face was so white and grief-stricken that it tore my heart. I could not forget you!"

The brown eyes, wide and wondering, were searching his face; she said in a low voice: "You were there, that dreadful night? It was the night my father died. Mr Brownhill had come to fetch me home."

He nodded. "I realized that later, after we met again. That is why I never spoke of it before. Perhaps I should not have done so now. Forgive me!"

"There is no need," she said softly. "You say that you wished to help me. You have done so, Sir Piers, more than I can say. Until we met, I had been very lonely."

"I hope," he said slowly, "that you will never be lonely again."

The rain began to fall once more, large, heavy drops splashing into the puddles and pattering on the leaves. Piers loosed his hold upon her and glanced up at the sky, where slate-grey clouds hung low and heavy.

"You must go indoors," he said, "for this will be no passing shower. Try not to think too badly of the smugglers, Miss Tarrant, in spite of the fright you have had. If you are to stay in Sussex, I fear you must resign yourself to our lawless ways."

"I will remember," she said wistfully, "but I do not think it likely, sir, that I shall be staying for much longer in Sussex."

"No?" he said gently. "But do you not think that you might one day be persuaded to return, and even, perhaps, to stay?"

He took her hand and lifted it to his lips, but the makeshift bandage was still knotted about it, and so he dropped a kiss instead upon the inside of her wrist. Her other hand lifted, and the fingertips touched his for an instant in a fleeting caress.

"Yes," she said in a breathless whisper, "I think perhaps I might."

She freed her hand from his and turned and ran quickly along the path, while Piers stood looking after her. At the gate she paused to glance back at him, and then with a shy little gesture of farewell she slipped through the gateway and the high brick wall hid her from him. For a moment longer he stood there, and then mounted his horse and rode homeward through the driving rain.

9

The Hand of Treachery

For the rest of that day Charmian hugged to herself a new, secret happiness. It armoured her against Lavinia's ill-temper, enabling her to disregard the scolding she received for arriving home wet and bedraggled, and sustained her throughout the almost intolerable tedium of the long, dismal evening. Had Mrs Fenshawe been less preoccupied with her own ill-usage she might have observed it and guessed the cause, for she could be exceedingly shrewd when she chose. So busy was she, however, bemoaning her exile from London to this dreary spot, and enumerating the many ways in which she could have been diverting herself in town, that she had no thought to spare for her companion.

Charmian was thankful when the time came to retire for the night, and darkness and solitude left her free to pursue her thoughts with no fear of betraying them to Lavinia. Lying in bed, listening to the sea-wind thrumming in the trees and dashing rain against the window, she lived again and again that parting by the gate of the rose-garden, treasuring each word like a separate, precious jewel. Not even the failure of her attempt to disclose the secret of Bell Orchard could lessen her contentment. She would speak of it to Piers again, more frankly, and this time he would believe her and tell her what she must do. She hoped that no serious harm would befall Colonel Fenshawe and his family. At that moment she felt kindly towards them all, for bringing her to Sussex and so making possible her meeting with Piers.

Her last waking thought was that if the weather had cleared by morning she would carry out her previous intention of visiting Wychwood Chase, but it proved easier to plan than to execute. Next day the rain was still falling, and it continued to do so with unabated energy the whole day through, until to Charmian, despairingly eyeing the leaden sky, it scarcely seemed possible that there was any left to fall. To venture out in such weather would be madness, and instantly arouse Lavinia's suspicions. Somehow she must find the patience to stay quietly indoors, to wait a little longer before sharing the burden of her knowledge.

Towards evening she was astonished to see a travelling-coach, plastered with mud and drawn by weary, plodding horses, coming slowly along the drive. It lumbered to a halt before the front door, and after a little delay, and a considerable hurrying to and fro of servants, there emerged from its interior a slight gentleman swathed in a voluminous cloak, who made great haste to enter the house. Several minutes elapsed, and then the door of the parlour opened and Miles Fenshawe came in.

He had divested himself of cloak and hat, and now stood resplendent in dark-blue velvet laced with gold, a froth of lace at throat and wrist, his wig exquisitely curled and powdered, and his whole appearance so immaculate it seemed incredible that he had just completed a long and uncomfortable journey. For a moment he regarded the two women in silence, and then made them a bow of marvellous and complicated grace.

"Ladies," he greeted them in his high-pitched, drawling voice, "behold me your most humble and obedient servant! I trust I see you both well?" He trod gracefully across the room and lifted his stepmother's hand to his lips. "Madam, my father sends you loving greetings, and his regrets that business of a pressing nature detains him at present in London. I am the bearer of a letter from him which will make all plain."

He produced it from his pocket and bestowed it upon her with another graceful flourish before turning to bow again before Charmian.

"My dear Miss Tarrant, there is no need to inquire whether you have benefited from this change of scene—I read it in your face. I am enchanted to find you so much recovered."

She made some civil response to this, contriving to hide her dismay at his unexpected arrival. It was not merely that she disliked Miles Fenshawe—if dislike were not too strong a term for the impatient contempt she felt for the young dandy—but also the fear that his chief purpose in coming was to resume the determined courtship which had so vexed and embarrassed her in London. Miles, she felt sure, would not allow the fact that she was in mourning to deter him, and with him constantly at her elbow she would have small chance of another private conversation with Piers.

Lavinia had been sitting with her husband's letter in her hand, looking down at it as though deliberating whether or not to read it at once. Eventually she put it into her pocket with the seals unbroken and turned again to Miles.

"I cannot tell you what a relief to me it is to see a fresh face," she declared. "Tell me, is your father well? What is the latest gossip in town, the newest mode? I vow, Miles, I have near died of boredom these past weeks. Come, sit by me and tell me all the news!"

He obeyed with every appearance of complaisance, and having assured her that Colonel Fenshawe was in the very best of health, launched at once into a spate of amusing and often scandalous anecdote. Lavinia listened avidly, her eyes bright with interest and her whole expression more animated than it had been for weeks. Now and then she interjected a comment or question, and more than once her clear, tinkling laughter rang out, but for the most part it was Miles's lazy drawl that dominated the conversation. Charmian, her head bent over her needle-work, listened with only half her attention, for though Miles was undoubtedly amusing and it was diverting to learn what was going on in London, she could not rid herself of the feeling that there was some purpose for his visit which was not apparent.

Did it, she wondered, portend some renewal of Jacobite activity? Was some secret agent to be smuggled in from the Continent, or information and promises of support carried from England to the Stuart prince waiting in France? She tried to picture Miles playing a part in such desperate and secret deeds, but her imagination proved unequal to the task. It was easy enough to visualize Harry doing so, but not his exquisite younger brother.

Had she been present at another conversation, which took place that night after she had gone to bed, she might have seen the younger Mr Fenshawe in a different light. She retired early, leaving Miles and Lavinia at cards in the parlour, and at this occupation they continued for some time after she had left them. The game was interrupted at length by Harry, who came storming into the room with raindrops glistening on his hair and clothes, and an expression of fury in his face. Lavinia jumped and dropped a card, but Miles merely raised his eyes for a moment to favour his brother with a mocking glance before returning to the study of his own hand.

Just for an instant Harry paused, his eyes narrowed beneath scowling brows, and then he strode forward and his riding-whip hissed through the air to crash down upon the card-table, scattering cards and coins alike across the floor. Lavinia uttered a startled cry, but he paid no heed to her.

"Attend to me, curse you!" he said in a voice thick with rage. "What was the meaning of that damned impertinent message you sent me?"

Slowly Miles raised his eyes again to his brother's face, his expression one of mock perplexity. "Why, was it not clear to you?" he drawled. "I thought it made my meaning abundantly plain, though, upon my soul, you have been in no haste to answer it!"

"I do not jump to your bidding," Harry retorted angrily. "You insufferable puppy, I've a mind to lay this whip across your back to remind you of that!"

Miles continued to look up at him, a faint smile hovering about his lips, but when he spoke his voice was cold and passionless. "Do not attempt it," he said softly. "As you value your life, dear brother, do not attempt it."

"Harry! Miles!" Lavinia had recovered her composure, and spoke sharply. "For pity's sake, can you never meet without embarking on a mortal quarrel? There are more important issues at stake than the fancied slights you put upon each other, and I, at least, desire to know exactly how matters stand. Your father's letter told me nothing."

"As usual, my dear Lavinia, you show admirable common sense," Miles murmured, "and now that Harry has designed to tear himself at last from the arms of his rustic light-o'-love, I will explain to you both what could not be set down in writing." He put down the cards and leaned back in his chair, one white hand toying with the quizzing-glass which hung on a ribbon about his neck. "In the first place, my father is seriously displeased by this intimate friendship which you have allowed to grow up between Miss Tarrant and the Wychwoods. It is unnecessary, undesirable, and could be exceedingly dangerous to us all."

"Do you think I do not know that?" Lavinia said indignantly. "I assure you, I have done all in *my* power to discourage it! Her first meeting with Piers Wychwood was an unfortunate chance, but since then he and his mother and sister have gone out of their way to befriend her. Harry will have it that they know her to be an heiress, and hope to draw her fortune into their own pockets."

"Then for once Harry is very probably right," Miles replied in a bored voice, "but such a thing cannot be permitted to happen. It should never have been permitted to come within the bounds of possibility."

Harry gave a short, angry laugh and turned to Lavinia. "We are totally in the wrong, m'dear!" he said with heavy sarcasm. "When Lady Wychwood and Dorothy came to call upon you, you should have locked Miss Tarrant in her room and ordered them out of the house. I should have called Piers out and run him through! That would have discouraged them, and no one would have suspected that we have anything to hide."

"I suppose you imagine that you are being witty," Miles said contemptuously. "Unfortunately I do not find such schoolboy humour amusing."

"I must say, Miles," Lavinia put in hastily, "that I feel you and your father are being a trifle unjust. Harry exaggerates, of course, but how *could* we prevent the association without giving rise to speculation? Piers Wychwood is troublesome enough already, and it would be fatally easy to give him cause to suspect us. We acted, as we thought, for the best."

Miles lifted the quizzing-glass, and through it surveyed his stepmother with some severity. "You display an astonishing lack of imagination, Lavinia," he drawled, "stap me if you do not! From Harry one does not expect finesse, but from you——!" He shrugged, and let the glass drop to the length of its ribbon. "However, it is of no importance now! *I* will put an end to this most ill-advised friendship. That is why I am here."

"Is it, b'Gad?" Harry said with a sneer. "May we ask how you propose to do it?"

Miles shook his head. "If a remedy so obvious has occurred to neither of you," he replied, "I do not intend to enlighten you. It will be done, and done effectively, that I promise you. Now, in the fiend's name, let us leave this and come to other matters! There are certain facts which my father desires you to know."

He had spoken with no change of tone, and yet his two companions knew instinctively that what he had to tell was not good. They exchanged glances, and Harry reached out to draw a chair up to the table, and sat down. The action revealed, more clearly than words could have done, that he was prepared, for the moment, to set aside his differences with his brother, and came to serious business.

"Concerning Rob Dunton?" he asked briefly.

"No," Miles replied, "not concerning Dunton. His whereabouts remains a mystery. We are aware that he had business with certain persons in London, and that he then intended to travel farther north, but unfortunately the names of those he intended to visit are unknown to us. However, he must have completed his mission by now, so, allowing him time to discover where Miss Tarrant is at present to be found, I believe we may expect to see him here in the near future."

"Suppose," Lavinia remarked, "he has guessed the nature of the trap you have set for him, and has left England by some other route?"

Miles raised his brows. "Without informing Miss Tarrant of what he knows? That is scarcely likely."

"He might have decided to send word to her by some-one else," Harry suggested. "As long as she is in our company, he knows that he would have little chance of approaching her himself, but a stranger, he would reason, might accomplish it. Still, we have little to fear! No stranger can enter this neighbourhood without Jack Godsall being informed of it."

"Precisely, which makes it necessary for her to remain at Bell Orchard." Miles glanced at Lavinia. "Does she receive letters?"

"Not without my knowledge, nor send any, either," Mrs Fenshawe replied cynically. "In that respect, believe me, no girl was ever more carefully watched."

Miles nodded his satisfaction, but Harry said impatiently: "Oh, to hell with that! What do you have to tell us, if it does not concern Dunton?"

"Nothing pleasant, dear brother, I assure you," Miles said sardonically. "It seems that we underestimated the persuasive powers of our friend, Piers. The seed he sowed when he was in London shows promise of bearing fruit."

Once again Lavinia and Harry exchanged glances, and the latter said shortly: "Damn you, can you put nothing in plain English? What do you mean?"

Miles looked pained. "Am I so obscure, or are you merely dull? I thought my metaphor exceedingly apt, but then I know so little of such rustic matters as sowing and reaping! Does one reap fruit? No, surely not! One gathers it! Perhaps—"

The rest of this mocking speculation was lost as Harry's fist crashed down upon the table and he said in a voice unsteady with anger: "Devil take you *and* your metaphors! Are you going to tell us in plain words what is amiss, or must I choke it out of you?"

"Your partiality, my dear Harry, for the more brutal forms of physical violence is appallingly ill-bred," Miles retorted acidly. "It must be due to the company you keep."

Lavinia clutched at Harry's sleeve as he sprang to his feet. "Stop it this instant!" she said angrily. "This bickering belongs in the nursery! Miles, what do you mean about Piers Wychwood?"

"I mean, ma'am, that Piers found at least one person in London who took seriously his talk of Jacobite agents landing here, and that was his uncle, Lord Corham. His lordship has since been pressing the matter in the appropriate quarters, and though it would be too much to say that the Government has been stirred to action, there has at least been talk of action to come. Our first intimation of it came when my father found it necessary to increase the amount of money he has been expending to ensure that Excise activity in this neighbourhood is kept to a minimum. A few days ago we learned that bribery is no longer sufficient."

"Not sufficient?" Harry was still on his feet, leaning forward with his hands resting on the table, but his anger against his brother had either abated or was being held in check. "You mean we have been betrayed?"

"I mean that we stood in grave danger of it. The man Winthrop got wind of what was afoot, and took fright. Smuggling was one thing, but when it came to treason, he wanted no part in it."

"Winthrop!" Harry said angrily. "I always felt that he was not to be trusted!"

Miles nodded. "The weak link in the chain! Unhappily we had no choice in the matter, since he holds the position he does."

"Miles!" Lavinia spoke sharply, "you say 'we *stood* in grave danger'. Do we still?"

"I think not! Winthrop lacks wit as well as courage, and instead of selling his information to those above him, came whining to my father that we had deceived him. From his point of view, that was a mistake." He paused, swinging his quizzing-glass to and fro at the end of its ribbon, his gaze reflectively following it. "One might say," he added pensively, "a *fatal* mistake."

An uneasy silence fell upon the room. Lavinia sat staring before her with troubled eyes, nervously twisting the rings with which her long, white fingers were laden, and Harry swung sharply away and paced the length of the room. Returning to the table, he said abruptly:

"I do not like it! We never intended this!"

Miles shrugged, his eyes still intent upon the swinging glass. "We never foresaw the necessity for it! My father shared your misgivings, until I persuaded him to abandon them, for when a situation arises, one must deal with it as best one may. It is the only way!"

Harry stood looking down at him, and though a frown still darkened his face, it was less of anger now than of perplexity. Perplexity, and some disgust.

"What a damned, cold-blooded devil you are!" he said at last, and his brother looked up to meet his eyes.

"I am a practical man," he replied coldly. "Bribes or threats may serve for a time, but when silence is essential there is only one sure way to obtain it." He yawned delicately behind his hand and rose to his feet. "This has been an infernally long day, and I am weary. I will bid you both good night."

He took Lavinia's unresisting hand and bore it to his

lips, and then strolled across to the door. Pausing there, he lifted his quizzing-glass once more and surveyed the silent couple by the card-table.

"May you enjoy pleasant dreams," he added ironically, and went out, laughing softly to himself.

The weather had improved a little by the following day, but it was still sufficiently unsettled for Mrs Fenshawe to crush in no uncertain fashion Charmian's tentative proposal to ride to Wychwood Chase. Charmian would have liked to insist, but, fearful of arousing Lavinia's suspicions, did not dare to force the issue.

She was not the only person at Bell Orchard who had formed the intention of visiting Wychwood Chase that day. Miles, emerging from the house midway through the morning, looked with disgust at the grey sky and wet, wind-scoured landscape. It was not actually raining, but looked as though it might do so again at any moment, and he did not relish the prospect of being caught in a sudden downpour during his ride.

His horse, a mettlesome grey, was awaiting him in the charge of his personal groom, and he looked it over critically before swinging up into the saddle. In spite of his dandified appearance he was an excellent rider, just as he was unexpectedly skilful with sword or pistol, but he preferred to dissemble these accomplishments and be known rather for exquisite manners and incomparable taste in dress. Most people shared Piers Wychwood's view of him, and believed him incapable of holding an opinion upon anything more serious than the correct depth of a bow or the design of a waistcoat.

Arriving at the Chase, he inquired for Sir Piers but was informed that he had ridden out. Apparently undismayed by this, Mr Fenshawe signified his intention of paying his respects to her ladyship and Miss Dorothy, if they would receive him, and so was presently ushered into their presence. He stayed with them for three-quarters of an hour, regaling them with all the more innocuous scraps of gossip current in London, informing her ladyship that he had had the pleasure of speaking with her sister, Lady Corham, only a few days before, and delighting Dorothy with several well-chosen compliments. Then, having gleaned the information that if he rode home by way of Wychwood End he would probably encounter Piers in the village, took his leave with every indication of regret.

The rain, which had hitherto held off, began to fall just as he rode into the village, but as he was fortunate enough to see Piers crossing the bridge towards him, he was able to make this a pretext for inviting him to take a glass of wine at the Wychwood Arms, on the other side of the green. Piers, eyeing him with the faint amusement which was his usual attitude towards the younger Mr Fenshawe, and of which Miles's resentment was as bitter as it was carefully concealed, accepted the invitation, and a few minutes later they were comfortably settled in the wainscoted parlour of the old inn.

For a little while their conversation was general, but as Miles filled their glasses for the second time he said, with the air of one who braces himself to perform an unpleasant task:

"I am devilish glad to have this opportunity of talking to you, Piers! That was my real reason for visiting the Chase today. In fact, it was my reason for coming to Sussex."

Piers, taking the glass held out to him, regarded him with frank surprise.

"You astonish me, Miles!" he said bluntly. "I cannot imagine any matter between us being of such importance that you would travel all the way from London to discuss it."

"No, I am sure you cannot," Miles replied ruefully.

"That is what makes it so deuced embarrassing. Oh, the devil! It is a curst awkward situation altogether." He took a few sips of wine, and then added abruptly: "It concerns Miss Tarrant!"

Piers, who had been in the act of raising his own glass to his lips, checked, and then set it down again with the wine untasted. His face had become suddenly very stern.

"I do not think," he said coldly, "that that is a subject I care to discuss with you, now or at any time."

"Unfortunately, my dear fellow, it is one which must be discussed. You are under a misapprehension which it is my duty to correct." He paused to take another sip of wine, and then added with lazy deliberation: "Miss Tarrant is betrothed to me."

He was watching the other man closely without appearing to do so, and saw with satisfaction his slight change of colour, the sudden look of shock in the blue-grey eyes. Piers said violently:

"I do not—" he checked, was silent for an instant and then added in a more controlled voice: "I find that difficult to believe."

Miles shrugged slightly and moved his hand in a small deprecating gesture, but made no reply. There was another, and longer pause.

"Are you trying to tell me," Piers said at length, "that this betrothal is of a clandestine nature?"

"My dear Piers, you amaze me!" There was faintly mocking reproach in Miles's voice. "Surely you do not suppose that either Miss Tarrant or I would stoop to anything so illbred? The marriage was arranged with all due regard for propriety, and with the consent of her father. Unfortunately he died before it could be made generally known."

"You mean, do you not, that he took his own life?" Piers said in a hard voice.

"If you must have it bluntly, yes, he did," Miles replied acidly, "but not, I assure you, because I was to become his son-in-law."

Piers made no response to this, and after a little Miles continued:

"You will agree, I am sure, that in the circumstances it was impossible to make any kind of formal announcement. Miss Tarrant has no relatives, and so it was decided that she should come with my stepmother to Bell Orchard until she has recovered somewhat from the shock of what has happened. In a month or two we shall be married quietly there, and I will take her abroad until her period of mourning is over."

Piers turned abruptly away and went across to the window, standing there with his back to the room. Miles smiled maliciously to himself and drank the rest of his wine. A minute passed, and then two, marked by the measured ticking of the tall clock in the corner.

"This is a damnable situation from every point of view," Miles remarked at length. "My stepmother did all she could to avert it, but did not feel at liberty to disclose the truth. That is why she sent for me."

"Miss Tarrant herself could have disclosed it with no fear that the confidence would be betrayed." Piers' voice was admirably controlled, but he could not keep it entirely free from bitterness. "She and my sister, I should have thought, had achieved a sufficient degree of intimacy for that."

"That, my friend, is the crux of the whole matter," Miles said resignedly. "It is difficult for me to explain without seeming disloyal to Miss Tarrant, but I wish you to know that I do not blame *you* in the least." He sighed. "No, I know only too well where the true fault lies. It was the same in London, even while our betrothal was being discussed. That air of shy innocence can be very misleading!" He paused, as though selecting his words with the utmost care. "Do not misunderstand me! She means no harm by it, and one must remember that she has long lacked a mother's guidance. Perhaps that is why she resents my stepmother's attempts to check her waywardness. I should have come with them to Bell Orchard, for she will attend to what I say, but I did not imagine that it would be necessary. With her father so recently and shockingly dead, I could not believe——! However, 'tis all made plain now, and I know that I can depend upon your discretion."

He paused again, but Piers neither moved nor spoke. Miles drew on his gloves, smoothing them carefully over his hands, and picked up his riding-whip.

"It will be best, I think," he drawled, "if even Lady Wychwood and Miss Dorothy are told nothing until after Miss Tarrant and I are wed. That will spare all of us a degree of embarrassment. Do you not agree?".

"Certainly, if you wish it," Piers replied curtly, without looking round. "I am not in the habit of gossiping, even with my own mother and sister."

"My dear Piers, I am sure you are not!" Miles agreed softly. "I will take my leave, then, but no doubt we shall meet again. I shall stay at Bell Orchard."

There was no response from the rigid figure by the window, and once more a smile of malicious mockery curved Miles's lips. He strolled out into the passage and called to the inn-keeper to have his horse brought to the door, for the rain had lessened to a mere drizzle. While he waited for his orders to be obeyed he lounged gracefully in the doorway, idly twirling his whip and gazing across the village green with a satisfied, reflective smile. He was feeling very pleased with himself.

For a long time after Miles had left him, Piers remained staring from the parlour window, though he saw nothing of the familiar scene before his eyes. His first reaction to Miles's statement had been outright disbelief, but a moment later had come the chilling thought that Miles had nothing to gain by telling a lie so easy to disprove. Here, too, was the explanation of the Fenshawes' concern for Miss Tarrant, which in a family as self-centred as he knew theirs to be, had puzzled him a good deal. No wonder that Lavinia Fenshawe, who hated the country, was now prepared to remain for weeks at Bell Orchard. The hand of an heiress for a younger son was an achievement indeed.

Much harder to believe was Miles's assertion that Charmian was a heartless coquette, ready to conceal her betrothal and embark upon a flirtation within weeks of her father's death. His first impulse had been to call Miles a liar, to tell him he knew less than nothing of the woman he was to marry, but then the memory of his own meeting with Charmian the day before had come to restrain him. Against his will, it convinced him that Miles was speaking the truth. He recalled her pretty air of confusion, her confession of loneliness, her shy, hesitant response to his veiled declaration of his feelings for her. He had not ventured to speak more plainly for fear of shocking one so recently bereaved, yet all the while she had been playing a part, deceiving him for her own amusement, careless of the hurt she inflicted and intent only upon making a fresh conquest.

He stood with his hands clenched hard on the window-ledge, and stared through the latticed panes at the peaceful scene beyond while a fierce tide of bitterness and pain washed over him. For the first time in his life he had come to care deeply for a woman, had dared to believe that marriage could be founded upon love as well as upon material and practical considerations. He had made a fool of himself—no, she had made a fool of him. That was where the deepest hurt lay, in the discovery of her worthlessness, and it had dealt a wound which would be long in healing.

10

Miss Wychwood Intervenes

Charmian's fear that Miles's presence at Bell Orchard would mean the curtailing of such freedom as she had hitherto enjoyed soon proved to be well-founded. By the second day after his arrival the weather had considerably improved; the pall of cloud which for three days had obscured the sky broke at last, and sunshine began to dapple the sodden landscape. Charmian thought it likely that Dorothy and Piers would come to Bell Orchard again that morning as they had done each day before the bad weather set in, but she could not curb her impatience sufficiently to wait for them. Knowing that if they came, it would be by way of the ford, and the bridle-path through the woods, she resolved to go to meet them, and sent word to the stables that she desired a mount, and a groom to attend her.

She changed into her black velvet riding-habit and went downstairs, fully prepared to find Lavinia waiting to challenge her decision, but to her surprise Mrs Fenshawe was nowhere to be seen. When she emerged from the house, however, she found not only the groom and two horses awaiting her, but also Mr Miles Fenshawe, elegant in a riding-coat of his favourite scarlet. She endeavoured to dissuade him from accompanying her, but he swept all her protests aside, declaring himself entirely at her service, and she was obliged to give in with as good a grace as she could. Perhaps, she thought, she could somehow enlist Dorothy's aid in diverting his attention while she talked to Piers.

Before they reached the edge of the woods, they saw Miss Wychwood coming towards them, but to Charmian's intense disappointment only a groom accompanied her. Dorothy greeted them with her usual liveliness and agreed without hesitation to Miles's suggestion that they should all ride together, but Charmian thought to detect a faintly puzzled expression in her eyes. She inquired after Lady Wychwood, and then, more diffidently, after Piers, and was assured that both were well.

"Piers could not come with me today," Dorothy added. "There was some business demanding his attention, which he insisted could not wait."

"Piers' devotion to duty is admirable," Miles commented mockingly. "I fear *I* could not emulate it, paticularly if it meant depriving myself of such charming company as this."

Neither lady made any response to this, Charmian being fully occupied by the effort of concealing her disappointment, and Dorothy wondering, a shade uneasily, why her brother's refusal to accompany her had been so curt. Miles smiled lazily to himself and changed the subject, chatting entertainingly upon a dozen different topics as they went on their way. He was fully aware that each of his fair companions was wishing him elsewhere, and was considerably amused by the knowledge.

On the three succeeding days the same pattern was repeated. Dorothy came alone to Bell Orchard, and she and

Charmian rode out with Miles as their unwanted escort,
an escort who skilfully thwarted every attempt at private
conversation. Charmian, certain now that Miles's only
purpose in coming to Sussex was to make certain that she
had no opportunity to betray his family's political conspiracies, and made even more uneasy by Piers' continued absence, was driven almost to desperation, while Dorothy's
misgivings increased as the days went by. Piers no longer
made any excuse for not accompanying her to Bell Orchard; he simply refused to do so, and even hinted that he
would prefer it if her own visits there became less regular.
She began to fear that he and Miss Tarrant had quarrelled, though when such a disagreement could have
occurred she could not imagine.

By the fourth day Charmian had been made reckless by
this continuous frustration, and by an unhappiness which
had very little to do with Jacobite plots. She made up her
mind to go to Wychwood Chase, arriving there before
Dorothy had time to set out. She ordered her horse half
an hour earlier than usual, but if by doing this she had
hoped to get the better of Miles, she was disappointed. He
was waiting for her, lazy and immaculate as ever, when
she emerged from the house.

She had learned by now that it was useless to try to
evade him, and accepted his presence without protest,
paying little heed to his conversation and searching her
mind for some excuse to talk to Piers, or even Dorothy or
her mother, without his knowledge.

When they arrived at Wychwood Chase, they found
Dorothy and Piers standing on the steps which led up to
the main entrance of the house. On the broad expanse of
gravel below, a groom was holding the bridles of two
saddle-horses, but the attitude of brother and sister suggested that a dispute of some kind was taking place between them. Both looked round when they heard the

riders approaching, and then Dorothy came quickly down the steps to meet them. Charmian, allowing Miles to help her from the saddle, answered the greeting somewhat at random, and cast a shy yet eager glance at Piers, who stood, silent and unsmiling, on the steps. The mere sight of that tall, broad-shouldered figure had the power, she found, to lift her spirits and dispel the fears that plagued her.

"This *is* a fortunate chance," Dorothy exclaimed brightly. "I was just about to set out for Bell Orchard, but my brother has to ride over to Bannerford, and did not think he had time to accompany me. We were just debating what to do when you arrived so opportunely. Now we can all go to Bannerford together."

Charmian's spirits soared still higher. Bannerford lay some four miles inland from Wychwood, and during the ride she would surely be able to contrive the opportunity she was seeking. She opened her lips to assent to the plan, but Piers' voice forestalled her.

"You will refrain, if you please, Dorothy, from making my decisions for me!" He spoke coldly, with no softening of his expression. "My purpose in visiting Bannerford is to inspect some farm buildings which my bailiff assures me stand in need of repair, and I am sure that neither Miss Tarrant nor Miles has the smallest interest in such a matter. You will do much better to take your ride through the woods or along the shore." He came down the steps as he spoke, and bowed briefly to Charmian. "Madam, your servant!"

He clapped his hat on his head, nodded curtly to Miles, and took his horse's rein from the groom. Mounting, he wheeled the animal about and rode off without another glance at any of them. Dorothy stared after him openmouthed, and Miles smiled thoughtfully as he drew the lash of his whip through his fingers, but Charmian turned blindly towards her horse again. She was trembling and close to tears, for as Piers bowed before her she had seen unmistakable contempt in his eyes. It had struck her like a blow, and if there had been hurt there also it had lain deep, and she had been too shocked to discover it. She said in a shaking voice to the groom:

"Help me to mount, if you please!"

He stared, but obeyed. Dorothy turned quickly.

"Miss Tarrant, wait! Charmian!"

"I do not feel well!" Charmian could scarcely control her voice, and said the first thing that came into her head; her eyes were brimming with tears. "I must go home!"

She paid no heed to Miles, but urged her horse forward along the avenue. Miles turned to Dorothy, lifted shoulders and hands in an expressive gesture, and then bowed to her with a murmur of farewell. Charmian was already some distance away and he was obliged to spur his horse to a canter to overtake her, but when he did so he reined in a few paces behind her and made no comment, giving her time to dry her eyes and regain some measure of control. He had achieved his purpose, and it was not his intention—yet—to twist the knife in the wound.

Dorothy, thus deserted by brother and guests alike, signed to the groom to take her horse back to the stables, and went slowly and dispiritedly indoors. Something was plainly very wrong indeed. The affair, which had prospered so greatly at first, had met with an inexplicable setback, and since she did not know the cause she was at a loss how to remedy it. She might have consulted her mother, but Lady Wychwood had gone to visit a sick friend, and by the time she returned Dorothy had recalled how discouraging about the whole affair she had been at the outset. She decided instead to take Piers to task, even if it meant his further displeasure.

In this intention also she was frustrated, for Piers

did not return home until late that evening, when Dorothy and her mother were about to retire for the night. He informed them curtly that he had been to call upon his old friend Tom Merrill, and was now going straight to bed. Since Mr Merrill's home lay seventeen miles beyond Bannerford, this plea of weariness was understandable, but Dorothy felt certain that he was deliberately avoiding her.

He continued to do so the following morning, and with mounting exasperation she decided to visit Bell Orchard again and make one more attempt to discover from Charmian what was amiss. She sent a message to the stables, and was in the act of putting on her riding-habit when Lady Wychwood came into the room.

"Dorothy, my love," she said, "you cannot go out today. I forgot to inform you that we are expecting company."

Dorothy paused with her coat half on, and stared at her mother. "Mercy on us, Mama! how could you forget such a thing? Who is it?"

Her ladyship did not reply at once, but paused to send Dorothy's maid out of the room. When the door had closed behind the woman she glanced dubiously at her daughter, who was regarding her with growing suspicion, and said reluctantly."

"It is General Grey and his daughter-in-law, and Selina."

"Oh, no!" Dorothy's exclamation was tragic. "Mama, how could you *do* such a thing, and at this time above all others?"

Lady Wychwood sighed and sat down. "It was at your brother's request, Dorothy," she said reprovingly. "He came to me three, or was it four days ago? At all events, it was the day Miles Fenshawe called upon us. As I say, Piers came to me and particularly desired me to issue the invitation."

Dorothy slowly took off her coat and dropped it on to a chair. "He means to offer for Selina!" she said in a voice dark with foreboding. "Oh, how can he be such a blockhead? Just because he has quarrelled with Charmian—"

"Quarrelled with Miss Tarrant?" her mother repeated in astonishment. "When, Dorothy, and why?"

"I have not the smallest idea," Dorothy replied, "but he must have done so, for when she came here yesterday with Miles, and I suggested that we should all ride to Bannerford together, he was downright uncivil to her."

"I cannot credit that," Lady Wychwood said severely. "Piers would not be uncivil to a lady, particularly if she were a guest in his house."

"Well, we were not *in* the house, as it happens, though that makes no difference. I own it is not like Piers, Mama, and that is what makes me so certain that something is very wrong. It wounded Charmian dreadfully. She rode away at once, and she was weeping. I saw her!"

Lady Wychwood sighed again. She was very much afraid that Dorothy had guessed correctly her brother's intentions where Miss Grey was concerned, and the thought filled her with dismay. She had observed his preoccupation with Charmian Tarrant, and come to the conclusion that one of her own dearest wishes had been granted, and her son found a woman who, besides being a suitable bride in every worldly sense, could also command his affection. Her disappointment was therefore profound, but Piers was a grown man and she felt that she had no right to interfere. A widow held the position of mistress of her son's house in trust only, and must be prepared to give place without rancour to the woman of his choice. If only, her ladyship thought wistfully, Piers' choice had fallen upon Charmian Tarrant rather than Selina Grey.

"I am exceedingly sorry if that is so," she said after a pause, "for I like Miss Tarrant very well, and from what your Aunt Elizabeth has told me, it would seem that there could be no practical objections to such a match. But you know, Dorothy, such a thought may never have entered Piers' head. A man may admire a pretty face, but he does not choose his wife for such a reason."

"But, Mama, Piers knows as well as we do that it would be an excellent match, and surely it is a good thing if there is mutual regard as well as worldly advantages? Oh, he is the most exasperating creature alive! I did so much want Charmian to be my sister!"

Lady Wychwood smiled affectionately and patted her hand. "Yes, my love, I know you did, but remember, Dorothy, you will yourself marry before very long, and leave Wychwood for a home of your own. Until then, you must be as pleasant as posssible to Selina, and remind yourself that she is the woman your brother chose to be his wife."

"Well, if it comes to that in the end, I will do my best," Dorothy promised with a grimace, "but I am not going to fold my hands and wait for it to happen." She picked up her coat again and put it on, buttoning it with a determined air. "At least I am going to find out why Piers has turned so suddenly against Charmian."

She did not wait for the protest she knew her mother would make, but whisked out of the room and hurried along the corridor and down the stairs. From a servant she learned that Sir Piers was in his study, but when she reached the door, the sound of voices within made her pause. She recognized the bailiff's deep tones, and knew that Piers would not welcome an interruption of business. So she waited, walking restlessly up and down, until at last the door of the study opened, the bailiff came out and, seeing Miss Wychwood, stood aside with a respectful bow for her to enter. She went past him with a smile and a friendly word, and heard him shut the door quietly behind her.

Piers, seated at his desk, glanced up as she entered, and it struck her suddenly that he looked older. In repose his face was always serious, but now there was an unaccustomed sternness in it, a faint frown between the brows, a certain grimness about the firm mouth. She felt a pang of loving sympathy, and spoke more gently than she had intended, though no less bluntly.

"Piers," she asked quietly, "have you quarrelled with Charmian Tarrant?"

A blankness descended upon his face, as though some intangible shutter had been drawn between them. He said curtly: "That is no concern of yours!"

"But it is!" Dorothy went forward and rested her hands on the edge of the desk. "Miss Tarrant is my friend, and I have a right to know why you behaved as you did yesterday."

"Very well, then! I have not quarrelled with Miss Tarrant. As for your friendship with her, that is an association which I would prefer to see ended."

"Mercy on us, here's a change of tune! It was by your wish that I first made her acquaintance."

"I was mistaken! I know now that Miss Tarrant is not a woman of whom I would wish you to make a close friend."

Dorothy opened her blue eyes very wide. "This is melodrama indeed!" she remarked. "Of what dreadful sin is my poor friend guilty, that we must shun her like the plague?"

Piers' lips tightened, and when he spoke there was anger, and more than anger, in his voice.

"This is no jesting matter, Dorothy! You will favour me by bringing your friendship with Miss Tarrant to an end."

There was a pause, while Dorothy studied him thoughtfully, and he made some pretence of looking through the papers which lay before him. At length she said reflectively:

"If I did not know you, and him, so well, I could almost suppose you to be jealous of Miles. It is only since *he* arrived at Bell Orchard that you have behaved so strangely."

Piers' chair slid back across the floor with a harsh, scraping sound as he leapt to his feet. "Now you are being impertinent!" he said savagely. "Upon my soul, your mother speaks truly when she says you are allowed too much freedom!"

Dorothy held her ground, looking defiantly up at him. "So I was right!" she exclaimed. "You *are* jealous of him! Oh, Piers, how absurd! She does not care a rap for Miles!"

"Be silent!" Piers said furiously. "I have borne with you thus far because I was responsible for your acquaintance with Miss Tarrant, but I will not tolerate any meddling in my affairs. It is plain that her influence upon you is already making itself felt, and the time has come to end it." He moved suddenly and gripped her by the arm, pulling her round the desk and thrusting her into the chair he had just vacated. "There is ink and paper! You will write at once, informing her that you will be unable to ride with her today, or at any other time. I have no doubt that she will take the hint, and not come here again."

Dorothy glared at him, and clasped her hands tightly together in her lap. "I will not!" she said with mulish obstinacy. "Next you will be demanding that I invite that odious Selina Grey to ride with me instead. Not that she would," she added irrelevantly, "for she is quite the poorest and most timid rider I have ever seen."

"You are acting like a spoiled and naughty child,"

Piers informed her coldly. It was plain that though he was still furiously angry, he now had his temper under control. "Neither Miss Grey nor her prowess as a horsewoman has anything to do with the present situation."

"Yes, it has!" Dorothy retorted wildly. "You mean to propose to her, which is what she has been waiting for years for you to do, and she will come here and make us all wretched, and you will regret it for the rest of your life! And I was so sure that you were beginning to care for Charmian, and would persuade *her* to marry you!"

Piers swung abruptly away from the desk and stood with his hands gripping the carved mantelpiece as he stared down at the empty hearth. Dorothy's words bit deep, stirring the pain which for days had been clawing at his heart, recalling the hopes he had cherished and which had been irretrievably shattered by Miles Fenshawe's lazy, mocking voice. He could endure her persistence no longer, and there was only one way to end it. True, Miles did not wish the betrothal to become known, but he had demanded no promise of secrecy, and what loyalty did he, Piers, owe to Miles or to Charmian Tarrant? After a strained and awkward pause, he said in an expressionless voice:

"That would be impossible. Miss Tarrant is betrothed to Miles."

"What?" Dorothy had been leaning forward to add emphasis to her words, but at that she dropped limply back into the chair. "I don't believe it!"

"Yet you may do so! I was informed of it by Miles himself."

For a few seconds Dorothy sat staring blankly before her, and then she said in a bewildered voice: "When did he tell you, and why was it kept secret?"

Without moving from his position by the fireplace, Piers told her, recounting briefly his conversation with

Miles at the Wychwood Arms. She listened with growing astonishment, and at the end said flatly:

"I still do not believe it! Charmian is not in the least like that, and to my mind the whole thing is a pack of lies."

"Why should he lie about such a thing?" Piers asked wearily. "What could he hope to gain, when Miss Tarrant herself would certainly deny it at the first opportunity?"

"But that is the whole point!" Dorothy got up and came to join him; her voice was eager. "The opportunity will not arise. Miles knows *you* well enough to guess how you will behave in such circumstances, and he has been very careful to see that *I* have no chance to speak to Charmian alone."

Piers turned his head and looked at her with a frown. "It is true," he said slowly, "that he suggested I should say nothing of this to you or to my mother. I wonder— but no! It is too fantastic!"

"It is not fantastic at all," Dorothy retorted. "Miles is the younger son, and we know from Aunt Elizabeth that Charmian is a considerable heiress. Depend upon it, he means to marry her himself, and you know that he has never allowed any considerations of truthfulness to stand in his way of obtaining something he wanted." She paused, her eyes searching his face. "Dear Piers, you do care for her, do you not?"

After only the briefest hesitation, he bowed his head in assent. Dorothy smiled, and, slipping her hand through the crook of his arm, pressed it affectionately.

"Then give me your word that you will do nothing ir-revocable until I have found out the truth. If Miles was *not* lying, I promise to end my friendship with Charmian and plague you no more on this subject. But if he was, and you discovered it when it was too late, you would never forgive yourself!"

Piers did not reply at once. Unlike his sister, he found it difficult to credit so intricate a piece of double-dealing as she attributed to Miles Fenshawe, and yet her suggestion had sown a doubt in his mind. That Miles was capable of such treachery he knew beyond all doubt, but in the shock and pain of the past few days such a possibility had never occurred to him.

His thoughts went back to the previous day, when Charmian and Miles had come to Wychwood Chase. The intolerable jealousy with which the sight of them together had filled him had provoked then only the desire to wound, but now he remembered the look in Charmian's face as he turned from her, the hurt disbelief so painfully reminiscent of the first time he had seen her, that night in London. If Dorothy was right, and Miles had been lying to serve his own selfish ends, then Charmian must be suffering as much, and more, than he.

"Piers, promise me!" Dorothy insisted, tugging at his arm. "For your sake, and hers, you must be sure!"

He looked down at her again, and she saw that he had grown very pale. "Yes," he said in a low voice, "I must be sure. My God! if Miles was lying—" he broke off, and laid his hand over hers. "Can you do this for me, Dorothy? If you can, it will mean more to me than I can say."

"I *will* do it," she assured him firmly. "Tomorrow I will go to Bell Orchard, and somehow or other I will find out the truth, even if I have to speak of this supposed betrothal in front of Miles. Who knows? That may be the best and simplest way. But, come what may, I will do it!" She squeezed his arm again, looking up at him with mischievous affection. "You will see, my dear, that even a spoiled and meddlesome sister has her uses."

11

The Man with Red Hair

Charmian rode back from Wychwood Chase in a daze of misery, and, arriving at Bell Orchard, fled to her room and flung herself, weeping, upon the bed. She knew that, to Miles at least, she had completely betrayed herself, but that fact seemed of no importance at all beside the intolerable hurt caused by Piers' inexplicable coldness. What had she done? What had happened to transform the gentle suitor of a few days ago into a stern-faced man who looked at her with cold, contemptuous distaste?

As she lay sobbing there she realized, with a growing sense of urgency, that she must somehow contrive to leave Bell Orchard. She had suffered more that day than bitter hurt. Whatever the reason for the change in Piers' feelings towards her—and that was a mystery which would torment her for the rest of her days—it meant more than the destruction of her dearest hopes and dreams. It meant the withdrawal of the only help upon which she could rely, her only protection from the insidious menace of Bell Orchard. Now there was only one person to whom she could turn for aid; her father's old friend, Mr Brownhill, at Richmond.

She got up from the bed and, drying her eyes, sat down with no more delay to write to Mrs Brownhill, trying to convey her own desperate sense of urgency without committing too much to paper. When the letter was sealed and directed, she rang for the servant girl who acted as her personal attendant.

When she came, Charmian regarded her with some misgiving. She was a willing but somewhat simple-minded creature who had taken the place of the fashionable maid Charmian had brought with her to Bell Orchard. Within a week of arriving there, Mrs Fenshawe had accused the woman of dishonesty, giving Charmian convincing proof of it, and dismissed her immediately. Charmian had made no protest at the time, but had since come to regard the affair as one more step towards isolating her completely, and now knew a momentary doubt of the wisdom of entrusting her letter to her personal attendant. Then, reassuring herself with the thought that no one knew what it contained and could not possibly think it odd that she should write to so old a friend, handed it to the girl with instructions that it was to be sent off without delay.

Had she but known it, her doubts were fully justified, for the maid, obedient to instructions which had been thoroughly and painfully impressed upon her, carried the letter straight to the housekeeper, who in her turn, delivered it to Mrs Fenshawe. Miles was with his stepmother when it was brought in, and as soon as Martha Godsall had left the room again, he took the letter from Lavinia's hand, glanced at the superscription, and then broke the seal. He glanced quickly through the message it contained, and laughed.

"It seems, Lavinia, that your guest has had her fill of Bell Orchard," he remarked lazily, "though I fancy that the outraged indignation of our friend Piers has a good deal to do with her decision to leave us. This is a request to old Brownhill to fetch her home to Richmond, and contains, moreover, certain dark hints that all here is not as it should be." He tore the letter across and across, and thrust the pieces into his pocket. "How fortunate, my dear, that our servants are so loyal to our interests!"

Charmian, ignorant of the fate of her appeal for help— for the maid, when questioned, assured her earnestly that it had been sent—resolved to wait with such patience as she could muster for it to be answered. Next morning, there being no longer any object in riding, she wandered disconsolately out into the garden, for Lavinia, who often lay in bed until noon out of sheer boredom, had apparently elected to do so that day, and Harry and Miles were nowhere to be seen. Charmian was thankful to be left alone, and for a time strolled aimlessly along the formal walks and pleached alleys of the old-fashioned garden, wondering wretchedly, as she had wondered all the previous day and for most of a sleepless night, why Piers had turned so suddenly and mysteriously against her.

Once, as she walked slowly along a winding path through the thick shrubberies at the edge of the garden, she had a strange and sudden conviction that someone was following her. She stopped and turned sharply about, but there was no one to be seen, and though she stood for some moments, listening intently, no sound reached her ears but the normal ones of a summer day. For a little she stood looking about her with a puzzled frown, and then with a sigh and a slight shrug walked on along the path.

It led her at length to a shrub-bordered patch of grass fronting a small natural grotto, where a spring bubbled among ferns and moss-grown boulders. This was the part of the garden farthest from the house, where the rising ground encircling the hollow lifted most steeply, so that the tree-clad slopes seemed to overhang the grotto and trailing branches swept low over it. It was a lonely and somewhat sinister spot, which had repelled Charmian the first time she saw it, but today it exactly suited her mood. She sat down on a flat stone near the spring and gazed wistfully into the tiny pool, and as though it were a seer's crystal, pictures formed and vanished upon it. Piers, riding with her through the sunlit woods, rescuing her from the smugglers, bidding her farewell in the rain by the garden gate; Piers looking at her with eyes cold with bitterness and disgust. Charmian bowed her head upon her hands and wept.

It might have been one minute, or five, before she became aware, in some subtle and uncanny way, of another human presence, and looked up through a mist of tears to see a man standing on the opposite side of the spring. For an instant she thought it was Miles, but as she blinked her vision clear she realized that the man was a stranger to her, a gaunt and shabby stranger in a rusty cloak, with a battered hat pulled low over red hair which fell, loose and unkempt, about his face. She was starting up with a gasp of alarm when he spoke, softly and urgently, in a cultured voice which contrasted strangely with his rough appearance.

"Do not be afraid, Miss Tarrant! I mean you no harm, and have come here as your friend."

She sank down again on the stony seat, bewilderment now mingling with her first, involuntary fear. At a second glance the stranger did not seem unduly alarming. He was about forty, she judged, of lean and wiry build, with a lined but not unprepossessing countenance. He looked, she thought, like a fugitive; weary, hunted, but not yet defeated.

"Who are you?" she asked in a quavering voice. "How do you know my name?"

"Who I am does not matter. I know your name because I have come seeking you, to tell you how and why your father died."

"My father?" she repeated in a whisper, and a nameless dread began to lay hold upon her. "My father took his own life!"

"Did he?" The stranger's question was sardonic. He came quickly round the little pool and dropped to one knee beside her, speaking in a voice no louder than a whisper, yet with an urgency which brought conviction with it. "Listen to me, Miss Tarrant, and pay heed to what I say, for if what I suspect is true, you stand in grave danger." She started to speak, but he raised a hand to check her. "No, let me finish, for time is short and I risk my life in coming here at all. Did you know that your father was loyal to King James?"

She nodded. "Colonel Fenshawe told me so, when I wanted an inquiry made into the disappearance of my father's fortune."

A sneer twisted the stranger's lips. "Did he so? That was a shrewd move, for an inquiry is the last thing he would want. I suppose he told you that he and his family hold similar loyalties?"

She nodded again, staring at him while that indefinable dread tightened its hold upon her, bringing with it a foreboding that as yet she had barely glimpsed the secrets of Bell Orchard, but that this man could lay them bare before her. There was no question of doubting what he said; a fierce sincerity burned in every word and look.

"A few weeks ago, Miss Tarrant," he went on, "I crossed from France aboard a vessel called the *Pride of Sussex,* which, under the guise of fishing, plies a brisk trade in contraband. Stealth was necessary because I came upon the Prince's business, and am too well known to the Elector's spies to enter England openly. Also aboard the ship were Harry and Miles Fenshawe."

Charmian stared at him. "On a smuggler's ship?" she repeated. "Was their errand then the same as yours?"

The stranger shook his head. "No, Miss Tarrant, it was not," he said grimly. "They were aboard that craft because smuggling is their business, the source of much of their wealth. Jack Godsall is known hereabouts as the leader, but behind him stands Colonel Fenshawe. He it is who bribes the Excisemen to turn a blind eye to what goes on along this stretch of coast, and it is not only in Sussex that he has Government officials in his pay. Even in London there are those who accept his bribes and see to it that any attempt to enforce more rigorous action comes to nothing."

Charmian continued to stare at him in astonishment, trying to accept the things he was telling her, realizing now why Piers' efforts to stir the authorities to action had made so little headway. She said doubtfully:

"But the Jacobites—?"

"Ah, yes!" Her companion's voice was bitter. "There, too, the ingenious Colonel plies a thriving trade. He will ship us across the channel, bring us secretly ashore, provide us with horses—at a price! That is his only connexion with our cause."

"Then how did he discover where my father's loyalty lay?"

"Simply enough! There are many places in London where English Jacobites meet to talk and make plans— God knows most of them do nothing more!—and for his own purposes Fenshawe frequents such places. That was how he met your father. He professed to share his feelings and then persuaded him to place his fortune at King

James's disposal. But not a penny of it ever reached His Majesty! It went no farther than Fenshawe's pocket!"

Charmian uttered an inarticulate exclamation and buried her face in her hands, her heart pierced by the thought of her father, the idealistic, unworldly scholar, tricked and cozened by Fenshawe's plausible lies. Without looking up, she asked:

"How do you know this?"

"As I said, Harry and Miles Fenshawe were aboard the *Pride of Sussex* that night. They were quarrelling, as they usually do, and I overheard them and so learned of their double-dealing. I resolved then to go straight to your father—for they had mentioned his name and spoken of his house at Richmond—and tell him the truth. That money had been intended for the King, and God knows he needs every penny he can obtain! And when they had bled your father white, they might well try the same trick elsewhere. I had to stop them!

"They took me to Godsall's cottage in the woods, and early the next morning a horse was made ready for me and Godsall himself set me on the road for London, but somehow I must have betrayed myself. Harry Fenshawe and his brother followed me, but I have had some practice in evading pursuit and managed to throw them off the scent for a while. All this took time, and though I reached Richmond ahead of them it was growing late, and by the time I discovered your father's house all was in darkness there, save for one window on the lower floor. I approached it stealthily and, looking within, saw an old gentleman seated at a desk. I attracted his attention, and, when I had satisfied him of my identity, he admitted me to the study by the garden-door. I told him my story, and he was profoundly and righteously angry at the manner in which he had been duped."

Charmian nodded in silent understanding. Her father

had been a gentle man, but sometimes, if the cause were
great enough, moved by a strong, quiet anger which never
spent itself in idle word or gesture; and this stranger's
story must have angered him as few things had ever done.

"It was about an hour before midnight when I left
him," her companion continued, "and he had then formed
the intention of going to London next day and denouncing
Fenshawe, even though it meant revealing where his own
political sympathies lay. The knowledge that he had ruined himself merely to enrich a greedy, lying rogue had, I
think, dealt him such a blow that he no longer cared
what became of him. He spoke of you, and thanked God
that, by the terms of your uncle's Will, you were amply
provided for, and said that before laying information
against Fenshawe, he would see the lawyers and make
certain that your future was properly safeguarded, so
whatever befell him, no harm could come to you."

Charmian shook her head, the tears running unheeded
down her cheeks.

"He did neither, sir," she said in a stifled voice. "There
was nothing, save for his debts, to explain why he took
his life."

"But did he take it, Miss Tarrant?" the man asked earnestly. "I do not think so! I can give you no proof of
what I am about to say. Thus far I have given you facts,
but my certain knowledge ends when I parted from your
father at the garden-door, and heard him lock it behind
me. Yet consider this! His intention to denounce Fenshawe was unshakable, and Fenshawe's sons had followed
me from Sussex. And an hour after our parting, your father lay dead."

She stared at him in horror, and said in a whisper:
"You do not mean that *they* killed him?"

"I mean that they had everything to gain by his death,"
he replied, "and that all they needed after that, to make

their safety complete, was my death also. They have been seeking me, I know, but I have friends who have contrived to throw them off the scent. I was determined to speak with you before I left England again, to warn you of your danger."

"But it is you, sir, who stand in mortal peril," she protested. "You can have no friends in this neighbourhood, and Godsall's men are everywhere."

He nodded. "I know, and be sure I shall not linger, but do not make light of your own danger. I heard one other thing that night aboard the *Pride of Sussex*. Miles Fenshawe means to marry you!"

She stared at him, and retorted with more spirit than she had yet shown: "That may be his hope, sir, but it needs two to strike a bargain. Mr Fenshawe has made no secret of his wish to marry me, and I have made no secret of my dislike of the notion."

"I spoke of his intention, madam, not of his hope," the stranger replied grimly. "There are ways by which he could compel you, and I believe he would not hesitate to use them. You should endeavour to escape from this place without delay."

"I had already come to that conclusion, sir, though not for the reason you suggest," she replied, and told him of the letter she had written to Mrs Brownhill. To her surprise the information did not entirely satisfy him.

"Letters can go astray, and in any event, Richmond is a long way off. Is there no one closer at hand whom you can trust?"

Twenty-four hours ago she would have assented at once, but now Piers had turned against her. Yet, however she had offended, surely he would not turn her away once he had heard her story?

"There is Lady Wychwood, at Wychwood Chase," she

said hesitantly. "I have some acquaintance with her, and her son is a Justice of the Peace."

"Then go to her, my dear young lady, go to her immediately," he said earnestly, laying a hand on her arm. "Ask her to give you shelter and protection until you can communicate with your friends at Richmond. If you do not, you may find yourself compelled to marry one who is guilty of your father's murder."

Charmian regarded him dubiously. "I do not doubt your sincerity, sir, but could you not be mistaken? It is difficult to picture Miles Fenshawe committing either of the crimes of which you deem him capable."

"Think you so?" the other replied grimly. "Well, no doubt he has deceived many with his foolish mannerisms, but to my mind, of the two brothers he is by far the more dangerous."

This was hard to accept, though Charmian was prepared to admit that the speaker was probably better qualified to judge than she was, but she felt certain that Colonel Fenshawe himself was capable of any ruthlessness, and that the stranger's advice to flee from Bell Orchard was sound.

"I will go to Lady Wychwood," she said abruptly. "Whatever the truth of my father's death—and I fear that will never be discovered now—it is certain that these people robbed him of his fortune, and no doubt they have a similar design upon mine. I will not spend another night beneath their roof!"

He nodded his approval, but said warningly: "Do not let them suspect your purpose, or they will seek to prevent you. Can you find some excuse to leave the house?"

"Yes, for I often ride to the Chase to visit Miss Wychwood, and it will occasion no remark if I do so again. But what of you, sir? Your danger is more pressing than mine."

"Oh, I will find somewhere to lie hidden until dark, and then slip away." He rose to his feet, and bowed with a grace which belied his shabby appearance. "Good-bye, Miss Tarrant! His Majesty shall hear of your father's sacrifice."

"Good-bye to you, sir, and my thanks for your warning," she replied quietly. "Rest assured that none of your enemies will receive any aid from me."

He bowed again, and then turned away to the steep slope behind the grotto and clambered up it to disappear from her sight among the trees. Charmian stayed where she was, trying to accustom her mind to all that the stranger had told her and knowing that her presentiment of danger had been no idle fancy. Knowing, too, that she would find safety at Wychwood Chase. Whatever the reason for Piers' sudden coldness, it was not in his nature to deny help to any who needed it.

Suddenly, high up on the slope above her, someone whistled shrilly, a clear, compelling call, thrice repeated, that brought her to her feet in sudden, indefinable alarm. A moment later there was a scrambling sound among the trees and undergrowth, a shower of loose earth pattered down, and then the man with red hair half-leapt, half-fell down the last few yards of the slope, to land in an ungainly heap beside the spring. Something flew from his hand and splashed into the pool.

"Miles Fenshawe!" he gasped as Charmian rushed to his aid. "He saw me, and I dared not risk a shot for fear of bringing others upon us!" He tried to rise, but collapsed again with a gasp of pain. "Damnation! I cannot set my foot to the ground! Where is my pistol?"

Silently Charmian pointed to the spring. At the bottom of the pool, plainly visible through the still rippled water, the weapon lay lost and useless. He blenched, but the next instant was looking again at her as she knelt beside him, and his hand gripped her arm with painful urgency.

"Quick! Into the bushes yonder and make no sound! If he finds us together, you are lost!"

"But you—" she was beginning, but he cut the protest short.

"You can do nothing for me! Hide yourself!" The whistle sounded again, closer now, and this time was answered from the direction of the garden. "They are all about us! Go, in God's name!"

Unwillingly she obeyed him, thrusting her way desperately into the thick shrubbery surrounding the lawn, hampered by the bulk of her hooped skirts and hearing the silk rip as the branches clawed at it. Crouching down beneath the sheltering leaves, she peered between them at the open space she had left, and saw the fugitive drag himself painfully upright, throwing all his weight upon one foot, as Harry Fenshawe appeared in the opening of the path which led to the garden. He halted there, and she saw, with an odd feeling of shock, the levelled pistol in his hand.

"Don't move, my friend!" he said grimly. "We have waited a long while for you to walk into the trap."

The other man shrugged, and spread out his hands to show that they were empty. "And now that I have," he retorted boldly, "no doubt you will slaughter me as you slaughtered the man you deceived and cheated."

A scowl darkened Harry's face. "I am no murderer," he said curtly, "though I could kill you now and swear afterwards that you set upon me. I have a right to be here, and you have not."

He paused as his brother came sliding and scrambling down the slope, to swing himself on to the lawn with the aid of a trailing branch. In his right hand he carried a naked sword.

Through a gap in the leaves Charmian could see the three men plainly, like a picture in a leafy frame, the Jacobite facing Harry, and the levelled pistol, while Miles paused behind him, sword in hand. What followed happened so swiftly that it was a second or two before she could believe the evidence of her eyes. She saw Miles's arm draw back, saw the unerring forward lunge, and the shabby figure of the fugitive give one convulsive jerk before sliding to the ground like a puppet whose strings are cut. She heard Harry curse in anger and protest, and then, as Miles wrenched free the reddened blade and stood looking down at the crumpled thing at his feet, the horror of what she had seen rushed sickeningly upon her. A shuddering cry broke from her lips, and she sank senseless to the ground beneath the leafy branches.

12

Bonds of Terror

The sound of that faint cry checked Harry's recriminations on the point of utterance. For a moment the brothers stared at each other, and then Harry dropped his pistol into his pocket and strode forward to thrust his way into the bushes. Miles turned slowly to watch him, his expression betraying no more than a mild curiosity, which did not change even when Harry reappeared with Charmian's inert figure in his arms. He stood, the point of his sword resting lightly on the ground, and looked thoughtfully at the unconscious girl.

"So we silenced Rob Dunton just a little too late!" he said softly. "A pity!"

"A pity!" Harry exclaimed explosively. "Is that all you can find to say? Damn it, man! do you not realize that she must have seen all that happened?"

"Naturally, and I realize also that she must be secure within her room before she comes to her senses and starts to babble of it. Take her back to the house, and tell Lavinia not to leave her, or to let any servant come near her, until we have decided what is to be done. I will deal with this!" He touched Dunton's body delicately with the toe of one polished boot.

Harry scowled, and glanced down at the limp, dishevelled figure in his arms. "How the devil am I to account for her being in this state?"

"Say that she has been taken ill, that you found her lying in a swoon." Miles bent to wipe his sword on a fold of the dead man's cloak, and returned it to its sheath. "Gad'slife! Have you no ingenuity?"

Harry glared at him, but realized that this was not the time to start a quarrel. He swung round and carried his burden quickly back towards the house, silently cursing his brother and the plight in which they now found themselves. A startled servant met him in the hall, but was brushed aside and curtly ordered to fetch Mrs Fenshawe, while Harry bore Miss Tarrant up the stairs to her own room. He laid her down on the bed and stood regarding her with a frown until Lavinia came hurrying in, a loose robe of flowered silk over her petticoats and her hair half-dressed. Her maid was close at her heels.

"What is it?" Lavinia demanded querulously. "What has happened?"

"I fear Miss Tarrant has been taken ill," Harry answered as she reached his side. "I found her lying senseless in the garden." Under his breath he added: "Get rid of that confounded woman!"

She cast him one sharp, inquiring glance, and read that in his face which demanded instant, unquestioning obedience. Bending over Charmian, she said briskly to the maid.

"Maria, fetch my smelling-salts and the hartshorn from my bed-chamber. I will look after Miss Tarrant." She waited until the woman had gone, and then added sharply to Harry: "Well?"

In a few brief words he told her. She turned pale, and

sank down on the edge of the bed, looking at him with frightened eyes.

"More bloodshed! My God, Harry! where is it going to end?"

"With our necks in a noose, if *she* ever has an opportunity to tell what she has seen," he replied grimly. "And how can we stop her, short of killing her also?"

"No!" Lavinia's denial was immediate and horrified, but her next words showed the selfish thought behind it. "It would be discovered, and besides, there is the money to think of!"

He cast her a look of contempt, and turned quickly to the bed as Charmian moaned and stirred. Her eyes opened, blank at first and then darkening with remembered horror, and her lips parted for a scream, but before she could utter a sound one of Harry's hands was across her mouth and the other pinning her to the bed. To Lavinia he said between his teeth:

"Get outside and stop that woman of yours from coming in! If she sees her now, we are lost!" To Charmian he added: "Be still and quiet, and no harm will come to you."

Her only response was to struggle more frantically than ever, but her strength was no match for his. Lavinia, hearing her maid returning, flew across to the door, checked there, and emerged more soberly into the corridor. Her voice, with only the faintest note of perturbation ruffling it, came clearly to their ears.

"You may give those things to me, Maria! Miss Tarrant begins to recover, and I shall not need your assistance. I will send for you when I need you again."

She came back into the room and shut the door. Harry said softly over his shoulder:

"Find me something with which I can gag and bind

her—something soft that will leave no mark. 'Tis the only way to keep her quiet until we have decided what to do."

In silence she obeyed him, finding a fichu of soft lawn for a gag, and ripping a silken underskirt into strips to serve as bonds. When at length Charmian lay helpless, bound hand and foot, Harry drew the curtains close about the bed and said grimly to Lavinia:

"If any remark is made, you must say that she is resting. Lock the door and keep the key with you."

She nodded, and when this had been done, they made their way downstairs. Miles, waiting for them in the parlour, greeted them with a look of bland inquiry.

"All is well so far," Harry said curtly in reply, and told him briefly what had been done, adding in conclusion: "It will not serve for more than a few hours, though, and after that, God knows what we are to do! Why in hell's name can you not curb your infernal lust for killing?"

"My dear Harry, you would make me out to be the veriest monster!" Miles protested mockingly. "I did what had to be done, that is all!"

"The one sure way! I know!" Harry said with a sneer. "But what use to dispose of one threat if it means setting another, and more dangerous one in its place? Or do you intend to silence the girl as you silenced her father and Dunton?"

"Harry, for the love of God, have a care what you say!" Lavinia broke in fearfully. "What if one of the servants overheard you? Miles, are you sure that you have concealed—everything—securely?"

"Yes, in the undergrowth behind the grotto. After dark we can find a more permanent hiding place for it. The river should serve well enough."

He leaned back in his chair, crossing one leg over the other, and studied his two companions. Harry was standing by the empty fireplace, one elbow on the mantelpiece and the other hand thrust deep into his breeches' pocket as he scowled uneasily before him; Lavinia, pacing agitatedly to and fro, paused now and then to push back the strands of pale blonde hair which, inadequately fastened, kept falling against her cheek. Miles smiled faintly.

"The situation is not nearly as serious as you suppose," he said softly. "It means altering my plans a trifle, that is all."

"*Your* plans!" The strain under which Lavinia was labouring was apparent in her voice. "How long, may I ask, has the making of plans and decisions rested with you? That is your father's privilege! Oh, why did he not come to Sussex himself?"

"Because, my dear ma'am, he is, as I told you, fully occupied in looking after our interests in London. As for my plans, they have his full knowledge and consent."

"Then what the devil are they?" Harry demanded bluntly. "You'll allow, I suppose, that Lavinia and I have a right to know?"

"Of course, dear brother, of course!" Miles assented smoothly. "But first tell me one thing. When do you look to see the *Pride of Sussex* again?"

"Within the week, if the weather serves. Why?"

"Excellent!" Miles said with satisfaction, ignoring his brother's question. "And within the week, Miss Tarrant will have attained her twenty-first birthday and will be her own mistress, free to marry as she chooses, asking permission from nobody. What could be better?"

They both stared at him, and Lavinia said blankly: "You are not fool enough to think that you can persuade her to marry you, after what she saw today and what Dunton must have told her?"

"Persuade?" he repeated, and laughed. "That is not, perhaps, the most appropriate word. I think, however, that when Miss Tarrant finds herself in France, without money, and with no means of communicating with her friends, she will see the wisdom of marrying me. The alternative, of being abandoned in such a situation, would be even more unpleasant, would it not?"

Harry continued to scowl at him in silence, but Lavinia said dubiously: "France is a Catholic country. How will you find a minister to perform the marriage?"

Miles shrugged. "If I can find none in France, we must travel on to some Protestant state. Remember, the farther we go from England, and the longer the wedding is delayed, the more anxious the lady will grow for it to take place."

Harry made an abrupt movement, as though dissociating himself from his brother's schemes, and said with a touch of scorn: "All very fine, but you are not in France yet, and we cannot keep the girl gagged and bound for a week. Even to confine her to her room will make the servants suspicious."

"But I do not propose to use anything as crude as ropes or gags," Miles drawled in reply. "Old Granny Godsall boasts that she can brew potions to meet any requirements, so let her now prove her skill, and furnish us with one which will keep Miss Tarrant sufficiently stupefied to prevent her from betraying us. As for the servants, they already believe her to be ill, having seen you carry her unconscious into the house, and if we hint that she is suffering from some kind of mental disorder, they will not think it strange that she is kept locked in her room."

"Who is to look after her?" Harry demanded. "If she is supposed to be ill, some show of nursing her will have to be made."

"We shall be obliged to take the Godsalls partly into our confidence," Miles replied. "Tell them that she has discovered our connexion with the smugglers, and that if she succeeds in carrying the news to Wychwood Chase it will mean the end of a very profitable business. They already believe that Piers is seeking to put down smuggling in these parts. As for looking after Miss Tarrant, Lavinia and Martha between them must attend to that. If no one else is allowed to approach her, it will add colour to the tale that she is mentally afflicted."

"That may be sufficient to dupe the servants," Lavinia said dubiously, "but what if Piers Wychwood or his sister come to visit her?"

"Piers will not," Miles said with a laugh. "I told you how he behaved yesterday when they met. If Dorothy calls here, tell her that Miss Tarrant is too ill to see anyone."

Harry turned more fully to face them, both hands in his pockets now, his wide shoulders propped against the mantelpiece. His handsome, black-browed face wore an expression of profound contempt.

"Ingenious, b'Gad!" he said sarcastically. "But will it not provoke a deal of surprise when this poor, sick, half-crazed girl recovers sufficiently to elope with you aboard the *Pride of Sussex*? Or do you intend to make no secret of the fact that you are abducting her?"

Miles raised his quizzing-glass and through it regarded his brother for several seconds before letting it fall again.

"I have always maintained, Harry, that you lack imagination," he said in a bored voice. "Piers already believes, does he not, that Miss Tarrant is betrothed to me? Once I have her safely out of England, I depend upon you, Lavinia, to make a great outcry, declaring that I entered into the betrothal against the advice and wishes of my family, because the unfortunate girl is deranged—the servant's gossip will bear you out in that! You will add that, discovering my father's intention to prevent the marriage at all costs, I have carried my bride off secretly rather than give her up." He sighed with mock sorrow, and shook his head. "I fear, however, that our happiness will not be of long duration! A few months, a year at most, and I shall be back in England, a grief-stricken—but very wealthy—widower."

For perhaps ten seconds longer Harry remained where he was, staring at his brother with an expression which almost seemed to imply disbelief. Then with an inarticulate exclamation of disgust he strode across the room, and out of it, slamming the door violently behind him. Miles laughed softly, and Lavinia shivered.

"I can appreciate how he feels," she said candidly. "There are times, Miles, when I find myself afraid of you."

He shook his head, amusement still lingering in his face. "Needlessly, my dear Lavinia, quite needlessly," he assured her amiably. "*You* do not stand in my way!"

On the following morning Dorothy Wychwood rode up to the door of Bell Orchard, determined to get to the bottom of the mystery of her friend's alleged betrothal. The servant who admitted her ushered her at once into the parlour, where she found Mrs Fenshawe alone.

"Dorothy, my dear, have you come to visit Miss Tarrant?" Lavinia greeted her. "I am so sorry, but she is indisposed and confined to her bed."

Dorothy looked blank for a moment, but then brightened, for it seemed that this might offer the opportunity she was seeking to talk to Charmian alone.

"Why, then, may I go up to her room?" she said brightly. "I promise I will not stay long."

Lavinia shook her head. "She is sleeping at present," she replied regretfully, "and I am sure you would not wish to disturb her. When she wakes I will tell her of your visit, and convey any message you may desire to leave for her."

She spoke civilly, but in a tone which warned Dorothy

that it would be unwise to be too insistent. Trying to hide her disappointment, she said:

"Will you tell her, then, how sorry I am that she is unwell, and that I will come again tomorrow to see how she does?"

"I will tell her, but do not place too much dependence upon seeing her tomorrow. Perhaps it will be best if you do not put yourself to the trouble of visiting her until I send you word that she is well enough to receive callers."

"Oh, it is no trouble!" Dorothy assured her guilelessly. "I ride out almost every day, you know."

She left after a further exchange of courtesies, and rode home in a somewhat puzzled frame of mind, to inform Piers of the failure of her errand and to remind him of the promise he had given her. Next day she presented herself again at Bell Orchard, only to be met with a similar disappointment, but when, on the third day, she was again informed that Miss Tarrant was too ill to see anyone, perplexity deepened to suspicion. She asked a few innocent questions of the servant who showed her out of the house, and then, instead of returning home, went to pay a call on the nearest physician, who had attended both the Wychwood and the Fenshawe families for as long as Dorothy could remember. What she learned there sent her hurrying back to Piers.

She found him in his study, making a desultory attempt to deal with some correspondence, but he thrust this aside as soon as she came in and asked eagerly: "Well, what news?"

Dorothy shook her head. "Mrs Fenshawe still maintains that Charmian is too ill to see me, and bids me wait until I am sent for, but Piers, I feel sure that she is lying! When I left Bell Orchard I went to call upon Dr Benfleet, hoping that he might tell me how soon I could reasonably insist upon seeing Charmian, but he knows nothing of it. He has not been summoned to Bell Orchard for months."

Piers stared at her with a deepening frown. "That is certainly very strange," he agreed slowly. "One would suppose that Mrs Fenshawe would have consulted him—unless, of course, she has sent for some other physician."

"There *is* no other within twenty miles, and in any event, Dr Benfleet has always attended the Fenshawes, just as he has always attended us. I believe this is all a plot to prevent us from seeing Charmian again?"

Piers pushed back his chair and rose to his feet and went across to the window, where he stood for some moments looking out at the wide prospect it commanded. At length, still with his back to her, he said heavily:

"There is one possibility you have overlooked! If Miles *was* speaking the truth a week ago, and Miss Tarrant knows that he told me of their betrothal, she may wish to have no further dealings with us. The excuse of illness may be a deliberate pretence, to avoid seeing you when you call."

"But it is not all pretence," Dorothy said triumphantly. "One of the servants told me that four days ago, Charmian was discovered lying in the garden in a swoon. Harry found her and brought her back to the house, and ever since she has not left her room, and only Mrs Fenshawe and Martha Godsall have seen her."

He turned, and regarded her with an expression in which concern was mingled with disbelief. Dorothy, having been so often taken to task for permitting imagination to get the better of common sense, hesitated for a moment, but then, emboldened by his silence, proceeded to expound her theory.

"Piers, suppose—just suppose—that Miles was lying to you that day, and Charmian learned of it. Perhaps Harry told her, to spite his brother, for you know they are always at cross purposes. It distressed her so much that she fainted, and now they are keeping her prisoner and pretending that she is ill, to prevent you from discovering the truth until it is too late."

He made an impatient movement. "That is ridiculous! What is more, it is impossible! They could not hope to keep her prisoner indefinitely."

"No," Dorothy retorted defiantly, "but they might threaten to do so until she agreed to marry Miles."

Piers turned back to the window again, and stood staring out while his natural common sense struggled against an unreasonable, growing anxiety. It was all wildly improbable, and yet there was just a remote possibility that Dorothy's suggestion contained a grain of truth. Miles Fenshawe was totally unscrupulous. He was the most completely selfish person Piers had ever known, and if he wanted a thing he would take it, with no consideration whatsoever for anyone who might suffer in the process. In Miles Fenshawe's world the only person who mattered was Miles himself.

If he had determined to make himself master of Charmian's fortune, he would have seen the threat to his plans in her growing friendship with Piers, and might have been goaded into taking a reckless step. Of course Charmian could not be kept prisoner indefinitely, but there were ways in which she could be compelled to agree to the marriage, and if she persisted in a refusal Miles was not likely to stop short at threats.

"There is one thing I have not yet told you," Dorothy said hesitantly after a pause, and something in her voice made him turn to face her again. "It is so absurd that all the rest *must* be untrue also. The servant told me that Martha Godsall says Charmian is going out of her mind."

"Servants' gossip!" Piers exclaimed contemptuously, but his uneasiness increased. It was plain that something very odd was going on at Bell Orchard. "Nevertheless, I think I will come with you tomorrow when you go to call on Mrs Fenshawe."

On the following morning, Lavinia was in Charmian's room, standing by the bed and looking down a little uneasily at its occupant. Granny Godsall's potion had certainly had the desired effect. For most of the time Charmian remained in a heavy stupor, now lying like one dead, now writhing and crying out in the grip of some nightmare. Even when, as at present, she was awake, she seemed dazed and confused, her mind still tormented by the horror of what she had seen and what Rob Dunton had told her—memories which she seemed scarcely able to distinguish from present reality. At first, Mrs Fenshawe had been completely satisfied, but now she was beginning to wonder how much longer they might safely continue to administer the sinister concoction provided by the old woman. Charmian looked exceedingly ill; perhaps the stuff was more deadly than they supposed. If the girl were to die . . .

Lavinia turned, picked up the glass containing the next dose of the drug, then hesitated and set it down again. Greedy and selfish though she was, she shrank from the possibility of becoming a murderess. Charmian was lying quite still, staring up at her with frightened eyes, and Lavinia was filled with sudden, angry impatience. All very fine for Miles to issue his orders; he was not obliged to force the hateful draught down the throat of this helpless, terrified girl. Nor, she reflected grimly, would it cause him the smallest qualm if he was.

There was a soft tap at the door, and then it opened to admit Martha Godsall, a big, coarsely handsome woman gowned in sober black. She looked frightened.

"Madam," she said urgently, "Sir Piers Wychwood and his sister are below."

"Sir Piers?" Lavinia repeated, her hand flying to her mouth. "What can he want here? Miles was certain he would not come!" She paused, biting her lip, staring at Martha with troubled eyes. "Very well, I will come down, and you go see if you can find Mr Miles, though I do not think he is in the house. Hurry, woman, hurry!"

They hastened out of the room together, and Charmian lay staring towards the door through which they had departed. Into the confusion and unnatural heaviness clouding her mind, their words had pierced like a ray of light. Piers was here, in the house. If only she could reach him, he would help her, would dispel this hideous nightmare which had held her in its grip for uncounted hours and days.

Painfully she dragged herself up into a sitting position, though every movement turned her sick and giddy and her limbs felt as though they were made of lead, so that the simplest action required enormous effort. But the instinct of self-preservation was strong, and somehow, little by little, she managed to drag herself out of bed and stumble barefooted across a seemingly unending expanse of unsteady floor to the door. Here fortune favoured her, for in their haste both Martha and Lavinia had supposed that the other would pause to turn the key. The door swung open beneath her touch, and the long corridor, floored and panelled in oak, stretched before her, an endless road which must somehow be traversed if she were ever to reach Piers, and safety. Haltingly, clinging to the wall for support, already near collapse but sustained by the two powerful props of fear and hope, she began to make her way slowly along it.

13

A Cry for Help

Lavinia found Piers and Dorothy in the parlour, and greeted them as calmly as she could. In fact she was a good deal more uneasy than she had been for many a day, and wished fervently that Miles were present to deal with the situation. Dorothy's tiresome persistence she had expected and could cope with, but her brother was a different matter altogether, for after his previous behaviour, his presence now could only mean that something had aroused his suspicions. She felt as though his direct and penetrating gaze was piercing her very thoughts, and looked away, afraid of betraying herself if she continued to meet his eyes.

"We have come to inquire after Miss Tarrant," Dorothy announced, and it seemed to Lavinia that there was a faintly challenging note in her voice. "I do so hope that she is well enough to see me today."

"My dear child, I told you that I would send for you as soon as that happy state of affairs was reached," Mrs Fenshawe reminded her. "Our poor Charmian is still far too ill to receive visitors."

"My mother and I were exceedingly sorry to learn of Miss Tarrant's illness, ma'am," Piers said courteously, "and if it is in our power to be of any assistance, you have only to inform us. It must be an extremely anxious time for you, particularly as Colonel Fenshawe is in London."

"You are very good," Lavinia replied, trying without much success to instil some gratitude into her voice, "and pray thank Lady Wychwood also for her kindness. It *is* an anxious time, but I am not obliged to bear the responsibility alone. Both my stepsons are here, and, as I believe you are aware, Miles has particular cause to be concerned in the matter of Miss Tarrant's welfare."

"Of course," Piers agreed blandly, "and I am sure that both you and he have done everything possible to help her. However, since Miss Tarrant's illness was so sudden and appears to be of so serious a nature, it does occur to me—if you will forgive the impertinence of the suggestion—that it may be beyond the skill of our good Dr Benfleet. He is, after all, merely a simple country physician. You have consulted him, of course?"

For a moment Mrs Fenshawe was tempted to say that she had, but perceived in time that a question so easy to put to the test might be in the nature of a trap. She shook her head.

"No, I have not," she replied with an affectation of candour. "The truth is, Sir Piers, that it would do very little good. Miss Tarrant's affliction was not, to us, by any means unexpected, for it is a sad inheritance from her mother, and was, in fact, the cause of that poor lady's early death. We know what measures to take, and there is nothing else that Dr Benfleet, or any other physician, could do for her." She broke off, pressing a handkerchief to her eyes for a moment before adding in a stifled voice:

"Forgive me, but the subject is too painful to pursue. You take my meaning, I am sure!"

"Well, I do not!" Dorothy said flatly. "I do not understand you at all."

"I imagine," Piers remarked in a dry, expressionless voice, "that Mrs Fenshawe is trying to tell us, as delicately as possible, that Miss Tarrant's affliction is mental rather than physical. Is that not so, ma'am?"

Lavinia nodded, and Dorothy, astonished that she should thus confirm the servant's incredible suggestion, said indignantly: "I do not believe it!"

"My poor child, it is natural for you to say so," Lavinia said sadly, "but I fear that you must believe it. You see now why I have tried to discourage your friendship with Charmian—why, in fact, we brought her to Bell Orchard. It is best for her to live in seclusion. Her mother was kept so, for naturally Mr Tarrant did not wish her affliction to become generally known, and when he was informed of the dreadful possibility that his daughter might have inherited the weakness, his first concern was to keep her, too, sheltered from the world. It is all one *can* do for her!"

Piers' level glance rested thoughtfully upon her. "Yet surely, ma'am," he said quietly, "Miss Tarrant entered fashionable society under your protection?"

If he had hoped to discompose her by the question, he was disappointed. She inclined her head in agreement.

"Yes, that is true! You must understand, Sir Piers, that at that time she had shown no sign at all of being afflicted, and it was hoped that she never would. But the shock of her father's sudden death, and the dreadful circumstances surrounding it, seemed to release the weakness which must always have lain dormant in her mind. For a time she was quite beside herself, and though she recovered after a while, and for some weeks, as you are aware, appeared as normal as you or I, this terrible malady now has her in its grip once more. I am told that it began so with her poor mother."

Still with that searching gaze upon her, Piers said, on a faint note of interrogation: "Yet Miles means to marry her?"

Lavinia rose abruptly to her feet and began to pace about the room as though she was too profoundly disturbed to remain still. She was beginning to feel pleased with herself, for though the idea of pretending that Charmian was mad had come originally from Miles, she felt that she had considerably improved upon it. She was almost beginning to believe it herself, and felt certain that she was convincing this earnest and meddlesome young man.

"He is adamant!" she said despairingly at length. "Oh, I will not pretend with you, Sir Piers, that I have not tried to dissuade him, and his father swears that he shall not be allowed to make so disastrous a marriage, but all to no avail. Miles is so deeply devoted to her that nothing will turn him from his purpose."

"Then his friends can only honour him for such devotion, Mrs Fenshawe, however much they may deplore the implications of it," Piers replied, and looked at his sister. "Come, Dorothy, it is time we took our leave. We have intruded too greatly already."

She stared at him in astonishment and dismay, and started to protest, but was peremptorily cut short. He turned again to Lavinia.

"Madam, I can only ask your pardon for what has been an unwarrantable intrusion into your family concerns," he said quietly. "The only excuse I can plead is that of ignorance."

"Pray do not reproach yourself, Sir Piers," Lavinia replied graciously. "I would, perhaps, have been wiser to take you into my confidence at the outset, but you can, I am sure, understand my reluctance to do so."

He assured her that he did, bowed over her outstretched hand, and firmly ushered his sister out of the room. They were half-way across the hall when from above came a faint, despairing cry that halted them in their tracks.

"Wait! Oh, please wait! Sir Piers, help me!"

Brother and sister spun round as though jerked by some invisible cord. At the head of the staircase, clinging for support to the massively carved balustrade, stood Charmian herself, barefooted and clad in night-attire. As they turned, she swayed as though the effort of attracting their attention had sapped the last of her strength, and sank to her knees, in imminent danger, it seemed, of tumbling headlong down the whole flight. Dorothy remained rooted to the spot with astonishment and alarm, but Piers strode across the hall and took the stairs two at a time, to gather the frail figure into the safety and comfort of his arms.

Seeing her thus closely, he was horrified by the change a few days had wrought in her. The light-brown hair fell tangled and unkempt, framing an ashen face in which her eyes, staring as wildly as the eyes of a trapped creature, were ringed by shadows as dark as bruises, and the hands which clutched at his coat were shaking pitifully. She was panting as though from some tremendous exertion, and the words she gasped out tumbled over each other, breathless and disjointed.

"Help me, for the love of pity! Do not be angry with me! They mean to kill me as they killed my father. *He* told me—the Jacobite, the man with red hair. He came to warn me, but Miles killed him, with a sword, from behind. I saw him do it, and now he will kill me, too. Oh, save me from him, please!"

Kneeling beside her on the topmost stair, an arm about her, he covered one of the frantic, trembling hands with his own.

"My dear, no one shall harm you," he said gently. "Do not be afraid."

"But you do not understand! They are not Jacobites at all, though they told Papa they were, and took his money for King James, but they kept it for themselves. Then they killed him so that he could not betray them. Now Miles says that he will marry me, but he is a murderer! He killed the man with red hair!"

Below, in the hall, Dorothy started towards the stairs, but Mrs Fenshawe, emerging from the parlour, brushed past her without ceremony and mounted the flight ahead of her. Charmian, looking past Piers' shoulder, saw her approaching, and with a whimper of terror clung to him more tightly than before.

"Charmian, my love!" Lavinia's voice was kindly and indulgent, the voice of one who reasons with a frightened, disobedient child. "You should not have left your room. What must your friends think to see you roaming about the house so scantily clad? Come, I will take you back to bed!"

"I do not think she has the strength to stand, much less to walk," Piers said grimly, and rose, lifting Charmian in his arms. "Show me the way, ma'am, and I will carry her."

"No! Please, no!" Fright and exhaustion combined now to render Charmian more incoherent than ever. "I must not go back there. They will kill me!"

Lavinia spread out her hands in a helpless gesture, and then turned, beckoning Piers to follow her. With Dorothy, a horrified and bewildered onlooker, at his heels, he obeyed, bearing Charmian easily along the corridor she had traversed with such painful effort to reach him. Martha Godsall, who had returned to Miss Tarrant's room by way of the backstairs, to find with horror that the door was open and the prisoner gone, heard their approach and came hurrying out to meet them. Lavinia waved her back into the room and stood aside for Piers to enter.

Charmian was sobbing hopelessly, so overcome by the failure of her bid for freedom, but as he laid her down upon the bed she flung her arms about his neck, clinging to him with the strength of utter desperation. Through her thin garment he was painfully aware of the violence of her trembling, the panic-stricken thumping of her heart.

"Do not leave me here, for the love of God!" Her voice rose hysterically in a last, frantic effort to convince him. "No one else can help me, no one! Oh, please, please!"

"No one is going to harm you," he said again. His voice was gentle, and so was the touch with which he disengaged her clinging arms. "My poor girl, you are in no danger, that I promise you!"

Mrs Fenshawe was close beside them, ready to frustrate Charmian's attempt to clutch at him again as he moved away. Holding the distraught girl firmly by the wrists, she said over her shoulder:

"My thanks to you, Sir Piers. Martha and I can manage her now, for there is a medicine here which will quieten her. Pray take your sister downstairs again, and I will join you there directly."

He nodded and went to the doorway, where Dorothy was standing, staring at the scene within the room in wide-eyed dismay. Taking her arm, he drew her out into the corridor and Martha Godsall shut the door firmly behind them, but as they moved away, Charmian's frantic voice came clearly to their ears.

"No, I will not take it! You are trying to poison me!" Then, rising to a heartrending scream of terror and despair: "Piers! Piers!"

Dorothy gasped and would have halted, but her brother's hand on her arm forced her on. Looking up at him, she saw that he had turned very white, and that there was a look in his face she had never seen there before, but he did not pause, nor would he allow her to do so. So they came again to the parlour, where she wrenched herself free and dropped into the nearest chair, covering her face with her hands. Piers stood beside her, one hand gripping the back of the chair, but he did not speak and it was plain that his thoughts were not upon her.

Only a very few minutes passed before Mrs Fenshawe followed them into the room. She went straight to Dorothy and laid a hand on her shoulder.

"My poor child," she said, "I would have given anything to prevent this happening. You see now what I have tried to spare you."

"I can scarcely believe it, even now!" Dorothy lifted a white, shocked face towards her; her voice was shaking. "Will she always be so?"

Lavinia sighed. "Who can tell? If her malady follows the same pattern as her mother's, this darkness will lift after a while and she will be as she was before, but it will return again, more and more frequently, until death brings the only release. If God is merciful, it will not be too long delayed."

With a sudden abrupt movement Piers turned away, but when he spoke his voice was calm and controlled.

"Once again, Mrs Fenshawe, we must ask your pardon and take our leave. If there is any way in which I can render you further assistance, pray inform me of it. Come, Dorothy!"

This time his sister obeyed him without protest, apparently still overcome by what she had seen and heard. From the parlour window Mrs Fenshawe watched them ride away, and then dropped into a chair with a sigh of relief. She felt exhausted, but satisfied. Charmian's unexpected appearance, her wild looks and wilder words, had convinced Piers Wychwood of her madness as no mere words could ever have done. In fact, although it had given her several moments of violent shock and misgiving, everything had happened for the best.

Dorothy was very subdued during the homeward ride, and they were approaching the ford before she spoke at all. Then she said in a trembling voice:

"Oh, Piers, it is all so dreadful, and I would never have believed it, if we had not seen her! Poor, poor Charmian! I could weep for her!"

Her brother, who had also ridden thus far in preoccupied silence, roused himself to glance at her. "Spare your tears," he said briefly, "for 'tis to be hoped she will stand in no need of them."

Dorothy stared. "But, Piers, it *must* be true! She looked so strange, so wild! And we both heard her accuse Mrs Fenshawe of trying to kill her!"

He did not reply at once, but put his horse at the steep slope leading to the ford. There was a set expression in his face.

"Has it not occurred to you," he said grimly at length, "that the accusation may be justified?"

This was too much for Dorothy, who had so often been accused of exaggeration. As the horses splashed through the shallow water she said indignantly:

"No, it had not, but what occurs to me now is that you have taken leave of *your* senses! Mercy on us! why should anyone attempt such a thing, Miles wants to marry her, not murder her!"

"Perhaps he intends to do both!" Piers said in a low voice. "*You* did not hear what Charmian said to me when I first reached her, before Lavinia Fenshawe came on the scene. No," he added as she turned eagerly towards him, "I shall not tell you what it was, for if it is true, then 'tis better that you know nothing of it. But this I will say—I believe that she is in deadly danger, and it is partly my fault. If I had paid heed to what she once tried to tell me, this whole damnable situation would never have come about!"

The fierce self-reproach in his voice kept Dorothy silent, preventing the questions which were hovering on her lips. As they began to climb the hill towards Wych-wood Chase, however, the full import of what he had said dawned upon her. She reined in her horse and said urgently:

"Piers, if she *is* in danger, we must go back at once! Oh, how *could* you abandon her in that heartless fashion, when she cried so to you to help her?"

He halted also, and turned on her with a white-faced, savage fury which was totally foreign to his nature as she knew it. Never in all her life had she seen him so gripped by emotion.

"You little fool, what else could I do? Did you expect me to carry her off there and then? Force my way out of the house and ride off with her across my saddle? A fine to-do that would have caused!"

"What matter for that? At least Charmian would have been safe, for Mrs Fenshawe could not have stopped you."

"No, she could not have stopped me, but she would have had the whole parish in an uproar before we had crossed the river—and the law would be on her side, make no doubt of that! Charmian would have been back at Bell Orchard within the hour, and I very likely facing a charge of abduction, and probably saddled with a challenge from Miles into the bargain. If I am to help her at all, I *had* to pretend to believe Mrs Fenshawe's story."

Dorothy, considerably chastened by these facts which, undeniable though they were, would never have occurred to her, hurriedly asked his pardon, but added miserably:

"You are right, of course, but Charmian is in no state to realize it. She will think we have completely abandoned her."

"Do you imagine it was easy for me to do it?" Piers asked bitterly. "To pay no heed when she cried out to me for help, to walk out of the house as though I neither understood nor cared? It was the hardest thing I have ever done in my life, and yet I had to do it. To betray any suspicion at all could only increase her danger, and if all that she said is true, then she is in mortal peril already."

"Then what *are* we to do?" Dorothy was almost weeping with frustration and dismay. "How can we help her?"

"I can think of only one way, and I had determined to use it even before we saw Charmian today." Piers urged his horse forward again along the winding path. "*I* have no right to interfere, and so I must find someone who has. I shall go at once to Richmond, to the old gentleman of whom Charmian has told us, who was her father's close friend for many years. He will know if there is any truth in this tale concerning her mother, and if, as I firmly believe, it is all a pack of lies, there will be cause enough for him to intervene. I shall ask him to return with me immediately."

"That will take so long," Dorothy protested. "Is there no other way?"

"None that I can think of. There is not one scrap of proof to offer in support of Charmian's accusation, and who, seeing her as she is today, would believe that it is justified? If we did not know her, and were not already suspicious, would we have done so?"

She sighed and shook her head. "I suppose not," she

agreed unhappily. "Oh, Piers, what can they be doing to her? She looked so ill!"

"That old beldam, Granny Godsall, could probably tell us that," Piers said grimly, "for I'll warrant the medicine Mrs Fenshawe spoke of is one of her damned witch-brews! But there is no hope of proving it. Godsall has no liking for me, and none of them would betray the Fenshawes." His hand tightened suddenly on the rein, so that his horse stamped and snorted protestingly, and when he spoke again his voice shook with pain and anger. "By God, I will make them pay for this, for all that they have made her suffer!"

He spurred forward again, and Dorothy followed him without further argument, but she could not help feeling vaguely dissastisfied with her brother's intention to seek aid from Mr Brownhill. To her it seemed a very tame and unadventurous way of dealing with the crisis, for her mind ran more to such measures as a secret, midnight entry into Bell Orchard and the spiriting away of the prisoner to a place of safety—measures in which she would have been more than willing to take an active part. But even if all the difficulties could have been overcome, she knew that Piers would never agree to so reckless a scheme. Not even the undoubted depth of his feelings or his consuming anxiety would deflect him from the path of practical common sense.

Arriving at the Chase, Piers sent his sister to tell Lady Wychwood what had happened, while he made his preparations for the journey to Richmond. These were brief. He took no servant and only the merest necessities, but because any appearance of undue haste would cause comment which might drift as far as Bell Orchard and arouse suspicion there, he casually let it be known that he was riding to visit his friend, Tom Merrill. Then he went to take leave of his mother and Dorothy before setting out at a leisurely pace in the direction of Mr Merrill's home, which fortunately lay upon the road he must follow to reach his real destination.

Once away from the immediate vicinity of Wychwood, however, the casual pose was soon cast aside, and it was a very grim and purposeful young man who rode northwards at a pace which would greatly have gratified his sister had she been there to see it. Only Piers himself knew what it cost him thus to turn his back upon Bell Orchard and the frightened girl who lay imprisoned there, deliberately to ignore the frantic appeal for help which seemed to ring still in his ears. To do so did violence to his deepest feelings, while the thought of the despair into which his seeming indifference must have cast her wrung his heart, but he knew there was no other way. The Fenshawes were as clever as they were unscrupulous, and for Charmian's sake he dare make no move against them until he was sure of success.

He rode hard, sparing neither himself nor his mount, hiring a fresh horse as soon as his present one showed signs of flagging, and reached Richmond in the early evening. He had little difficulty in finding his way to Mr Brownhill's house, but there a bitter disappointment awaited him. The old gentleman and his wife were away from home, and not expected back until late the next afternoon.

Piers was obliged to spend the night at an inn in the town, driven almost to distraction by the delay and by the thought of the ordeal which Charmian was undergoing so many miles away. Twice during the following day he went to the Brownhills' house, hoping against hope that they had returned earlier than expected, and twice was disappointed. On his third visit, however, towards the end of the afternoon, he found a coach standing before the door, and was informed by the servant who answered his knock that Mr and Mrs Brownhill had that moment arrived home.

Convinced by the visitor's persistance that his business was extremely urgent, the servant ushered him at once into the presence of his master and mistress, who had already been informed of his previous visits and were therefore somewhat curious. The name of Wychwood conveyed nothing to them, and both looked with some perplexity at this tall young man with the pleasant, serious face and air of quiet authority. He bowed punctiliously as Mr Brownhill came forward to greet him, to present him to his wife, and then to inquire, in a faintly puzzled tone, how he could be of service to him.

"That, sir, is a trifle difficult to explain," Piers replied frankly, "though it may perhaps simplify matters if I tell you first that I am a near neighbour of Colonel Fenshawe, of Bell Orchard in Sussex."

These words produced a greater effect than he had looked for. Mrs Brownhill uttered an exclamation, and her husband said quickly:

"Bell Orchard? Then, sir, perhaps you can give us news of a young friend of ours, Miss Tarrant, who we believe is at present a guest there."

"You believe?" A quick frown accompanied the words. "Are you not certain of it?"

Mr Brownhill moved his hands in an eloquent gesture. "We know that Colonel Fenshawe and his wife took Miss Tarrant to Sussex shortly after her father's death, and we received a letter from her soon after her arrival there, but we have heard nothing since."

"I have written to her several times, and received no reply," Mrs Brownhill put in anxiously. "It is not like Charmian to be so neglectful! Pray, sir, can you tell us if she is still there, and if all is well with her? We have been greatly concerned."

"Miss Tarrant is certainly at Bell Orchard," Piers replied, "for I saw her there only yesterday, but I fear, ma'am, that I can give you little reassurance as to her well-being. You are not her only friends to be concerned about her. That is why I am here."

She broke into dismayed and anxious questioning, but was silenced by her husband's uplifted hand. Mr Brownhill, shrewdly regarding Piers, said quietly:

"I believe, my dear, that we shall sooner know what is amiss if we permit Sir Piers to tell us without interruption. Pray be seated, sir! We are all attention."

Piers accepted the invitation with a word of thanks, and embarked at once upon his story. He told it in a deliberately calm and matter-of-fact way, but in spite of this they listened with deepening horror, and Mrs Brownhill was soon openly weeping. When he related how Lavinia Fenshawe had told him that Charmian's mother had died insane, she could contain herself no longer, but said with tearful indignation:

"That is a wicked, wicked lie! Mrs Tarrant died in an accident, poor young creature, as a score of people hereabouts will tell you. A team of runaway horses in the town one day—she thrust Charmian out of danger but could not escape it herself. Oh, that evil woman! I did not trust her, and should never have allowed her to take the child away!"

"Do not blame yourself, ma'am," Piers said grimly. "*I* have known the Fenshawes all my life, and until a few days ago I harboured no suspicions concerning them. Why, then, should you?"

"Such regret and self-reproach," Mr Brownhill put in, "is merely a waste of time which would be better spent in deciding upon a course of action. It is difficult to know how much of what Charmian told Sir Piers yesterday is true, and how much due to fright and disordered health, but it is plain that she is being kept at Bell Orchard against her will."

"I will go farther, sir!" Piers replied curtly. "Until it is proved otherwise, I shall assume that everything she said is true, and judge the extent of her danger accordingly. You will agree, I think, that there is no doubt that Miles Fenshawe means to marry her in order to possess himself of her fortune, which, I believe, is still quite considerable."

"Yes, her mother's brother, who was a very wealthy man, made Charmian his sole heir," Mr Brownhill agreed, "but there are certain conditions attached to the inheritance which may make it difficult for the young man to carry out his intentions. By the terms of her uncle's Will, Charmian forfeits all right to the fortune if she marries without the consent of the trustees before she reaches her twenty-first birthday."

Piers frowned. "You may be sure that Miles is aware of that! What happens, sir, if she reaches that age while she is still unmarried?"

"Then she becomes sole mistress of her inheritance and may dispose of it as she pleases. Naturally, when the Will was drawn up, it was supposed that she would be married long before such a situation could arise."

Mrs Brownhill uttered a cry of dismay and clapped a hand to her mouth, looking from one man to the other with horrified eyes.

"But Charmian is twenty-one this year!" she said in a frightened voice. "Her birthday falls on the seventeenth day of this month!"

There was a little silence, and then Piers said in a low voice: "And today is the nineteenth!" He stood up abruptly. "I must go back to Bell Orchard!"

"Sir Piers!" Mr Brownhill rose also, to lay a restraining hand on his arm. "What do you intend to do?"

Piers looked at him as though he did not really see him. He was very pale, and there was a grim expression about his mouth. "I do not know," he said quietly, "but if the time has already come when Charmian may marry without seeking anybody's consent, be sure that Miles will find a way to force her to it. If I am there, I may be able to prevent it." He paused, and when he spoke again his voice was unsteady. "By God! I *will* prevent it!"

Husband and wife exchanged comprehending glances, and Mr Brownhill nodded.

"Yes, you must return at once," he agreed. "We shall follow you with all possible speed, but we cannot expect you to curb your pace to ours when every minute is precious. Pray God you arrive in time!"

"Amen to that, sir," Piers replied gravely, and turned to take leave of Mrs Brownhill. She gave him her hand, searching his face with kindly, anxious eyes.

"Take care, Sir Piers," she besought him earnestly, "and may God bless you for all you are doing to help our poor girl. We have no children of our own, and she is very dear to us."

He looked down at her, and for the first time a faint smile took some of the sternness from his face.

"To me, also, ma'am," he said quietly, and kissed her hand, and then turned and went quickly from the room.

Within a very few minutes he was again in the saddle, spurring back the way he had come with an even greater sense of urgency than he had felt as he rode northwards. He was convinced now that everything Charmian had said the previous day was true, and the ugly word "murder" echoed constantly in his mind. If Miles Fenshawe had already killed in cold blood, he would not hesitate to do so again, once Charmian's fortune was securely in his grasp, and Piers recalled Lavinia saying of Charmian's supposed affliction ". . . death brings the only release. If God is merciful, it will not be too long delayed." Oh, they were clever, cunning as the Devil himself, and Charmian was alone and unprotected in that accursed house by the sea, so many weary miles away.

He was determined to reach Bell Orchard that night, and so throughout the long summer evening he rode southwards at breakneck speed, halting only to change horses and once, briefly, for food and drink when lack of it brought an ominous weakness and dulling of perception. Darkness fell while he was still a good many miles from his goal, but it was darkness made luminous by the light of a waning moon, and though it slowed his pace it failed to halt him altogether.

It seemed, however, that nature was determined to thwart him, for as he approached the coast, a thick, white sea-mist came drifting and swirling about him, pearly with moonlight yet strangely deceptive, cloaking even the well-known road in unfamiliar guise and forcing him to slacken to walking pace while anxiety and frustration rose maddeningly within him.

The nearer he drew to the sea, the thicker the mist became, but he was in a district now which had been familiar to him since childhood, and he was able to leave the road and ride cross-country, guided as much by instinct as by physical sense. So he came at last to the crossroads near Wychwood End, where the great tree spread its branches, and would have ridden on without a pause had his horse not shied at a sudden movement in the tree's black shadow. He curbed the animal with a firm hand, and then drew one of his pistols from its holster, saying imperiously:

"Who is it? Who is there?"

There was a moment of silence and stillness, and then a figure grew slowly out of the mist, resolving itself into that of a burly fellow in homespun, who said in a hoarse, placating voice:

"Bide easy, now, Sir Piers! It be only me, Clem Tappett!"

Piers relaxed, thrusting the pistol back into its place. Clem Tappett was one of his tenants, a farmer only a few years older than himself.

"What the devil are you doing, skulking there at this time of night?" He broke off as understanding came to him, and gave a short laugh. "Oh, no need to tell me! A thick mist and a calm sea—what could be better for running a cargo?"

"I'll not deny that, your Honour," Tappett agreed promptly, "but truth to tell, I be in two minds about having a hand in it tonight. Free-trading be one thing, but when there's murder abroad I'd as lief not be by."

"Murder?" Piers voice sharpened suddenly. "What do you mean?"

"Why, sir, have 'ee not heard on it? Two lads found a corpse a-floating in the river below Jack Godsall's cottage this morning. There were a rope about it, like, as though it had been weighted wi' summat, but the rope were rotten and had broke clean through. A stranger to these parts, so they say. A shabby-dressed fellow wi' red hair."

"The man with red hair!" Piers repeated in a low voice, and then, with a change of tone so sudden that his hearer jumped: "How did he die?"

"Why, that be the queerest part on it, your Honour! They do say he were killed by a sword-thrust from behind, but—" he broke off, the sentence dying on his lips, for with a sudden exclamation Piers had set spur to his fretting horse. The beast plunged forward, kicking up a cloud of dust, and vanished into the swirling mist, but Clem Tappett could hear the furious rhythm of galloping hooves, receding from him along the road to Bell Orchard.

14

The Place of the Witch

Charmian, when Piers had carried her back to her room and left her there with Mrs Fenshawe and Martha, had fought frantically to prevent them inflicting another dose of the drug upon her, but she was no match for the two determined women. The evil draught was forced down her throat, and because during the past few days she had learned to know and to dread its effect, all spirit immediately drained out of her. She collapsed on her tumbled pillows, sobbing weakly with exhaustion and despair, and Lavinia leaned above her, breathless and a little dishevelled, and said viciously:

"No doubt you think you have been very clever, but let me tell you, my girl, that you have destroyed any hope of aid from Piers Wychwood more surely than I could ever have done. Seeing you thus will have convinced him that you are ripe for Bedlam, and all you tried to tell him the sick fancies of a madwoman."

She straightened up and stood for a moment looking down at the huddled, defeated figure on the bed. Beside her, Martha Godsall stood with folded arms, stolidly awaiting her orders.

"I will go now to speed him on his way," Lavinia said at length. "Martha, stay with her for a while, and if she is troublesome, tie her up again."

She went out, and Martha seated herself grimly on a chair close by the bed. She would have had no hesitation in carrying out her mistress's callous instructions, but Charmian was too spent from her previous efforts, and too dispirited by the futility of them, to give any further trouble. She rolled over and buried her face in the pillows, overwhelmed by a despair so absolute that she could have screamed aloud had she not been too utterly exhausted.

Her hopelessness was made deeper and more bitter by her brief glimpse of freedom, by those few moments with the one person whom she had believed to be both able and willing to help her. Even now it seemed incredible that Piers had not believed her; that he had spoken with her, held her in his arms, and still remained unconvinced. Now she was lost indeed, robbed even of hope itself. Miles would take her, and force her to marry him, and after a little he would kill her. No one would be suspicious; they would think her death the natural result of her supposed affliction, and say that Miles was to be admired for his unfaltering devotion to a demented bride.

After a while she fell into an uneasy slumber, and Martha, satisfied that for the present she would give no trouble, left her alone, taking care this time to lock the door behind her. Charmian slept for several hours, a brief respite from terror and despair, which rushed upon her again as soon as she opened her eyes. For a little she remained unaware of physical needs, but presently she realized that she felt hungry. The discovery aroused in her a dull surprise, for Granny Godsall's potion had caused the mere

sight of food to fill her with nausea, and much of her
weakness was due to lack of nourishment. Now, although
she still felt wretchedly weak, her mind was clearer and
her appetite returning.

She pondered vaguely on the change, and reached the
conclusion that she was becoming so accustomed to the
drug that it was beginning to lose its effect upon her. The
discovery aroused a flash of hope, which died as soon as
it was born as she remembered her friendless state. Without help she could not even escape from the house, for
her gaolers would not be careless enough to leave the way
open a second time.

When, later, Martha brought her food, she was able to
eat almost all of it, and felt a little better, but no physical
improvement could lighten her despair. Rather did it
serve to increase it, for it would be easier, no doubt, to
endure what lay before her if her senses remained dull
and confused. So the day dragged past, and the night, and
another day, the slow crawl of the hours marked only by
periodic visits from Martha or Lavinia, and repeated
doses of the vile potion which no longer seemed to have
its earlier, overwhelming effect. Neither of the women realized this, for the failure of her bid for freedom had induced in Charmian a lethargy of hopelessness which
deceived them into supposing her still heavily drugged.

So on that still, summer night, when the house of Bell
Orchard was sunk in slumber and shrouded in swirling
mist, and Piers Wychwood forced his tired horse re-
lentlessly towards the coast, Charmian lay sleeping fitfully, plagued by dreams through which her father and
Piers, the Fenshawes and the murdered Jacobite passed in
tormenting confusion. From one such nightmare she
presently awoke to a reality more frightening still, to a
man's shadowy figure bending above her, and a strong
hand across her mouth preventing any cry. Convinced

that it was Miles, she lay rigid in a paralysis of terror, but it was Harry's voice that spoke in a whisper close to her ear.

"Not a sound, m'dear, or it will be the undoing of us both! You have nothing to fear from me. Do you understand what I say?"

She nodded vigorously, putting up both her hands to tug at that which was covering her mouth. It was removed, enabling her to say in a breathless, choking whisper:

"Oh, help me, please! Save me from your brother!"

"That's my intention," he replied in the same tone, "and there's no time to lose, for he means to take you out of England tonight. Do you feel strong enough to get up and dress?"

"Yes! Oh, yes!" Tears were choking Charmian's voice, tears of surprise and thankfulness at this offer of help from so unexpected a source. "I do not feel nearly so ill as I did a few days ago."

He gave the ghost of a chuckle. "You may thank Amy for that! She stole the second brewing of her grandmother's hell-broth, and replaced it with a harmless concoction of her own. I brought it from the cottage, and Lavinia never knew the difference. Now get up, and be as quick about it as you can, for there's no way of knowing how soon Miles may come for you."

He straightened up and moved away into the darkness, and she heard the faint click of the closing door. In a turmoil of hope and dread she did as he had bidden her, forcing her trembling limbs to obey the dictates of her will, spurred on by the fear that Miles might discover what was afoot and prevent her escape. She could not guess what had prompted Harry to come to her rescue, unless his action was simply one more expression of the ill-will which had always existed between the two brothers. Nor did she greatly care. The motive was unimportant; all that mattered was that he was prepared to lead her to safety.

She seized the first garments which came to hand, dragging them on anyhow in frantic haste, not pausing to struggle with the complications of tight lacing or whalebone hoops. She flung a cloak about her, pulling the hood up over her tousled hair, and then gathered up her trailing skirts in one hand, for with no hooped petticoat beneath they swept awkwardly about her feet. Tiptoeing across the door, she slipped softly out into the corridor, and Harry's tall figure materialized silently beside her. Without a word, he took her free hand in his and led her towards the backstairs. Descending these, they passed through the kitchen quarters and so at last into the open air, and the mysterious, mist-wreathed silence of the stableyard.

Charmian was shivering with mingled apprehension and fatigue, and her feet stumbled on the cobblestones, for the past week had taxed her strength more than had been evident while she still lay in bed. Harry took her arm to steady her, and guided her across the yard and into the stables, where he released her and moved away, and she heard the scrape of flint on steel. Then the faint gleam of a lantern dispelled the darkness, and he looked across at her and grinned.

"So far, so good!" he said softly, and pointed to an upturned cask. "Sit there while I saddle the horses. I am going to take you to Wychwood Chase. You will be out of Miles's reach there, and Piers will look after you."

She shook her head, weak, painful tears rising to her eyes. "He will not believe that I am in any danger. He would not believe it yesterday."

"He will now," Harry replied grimly. "They dragged Rob Dunton's body out of the river this morning."

"The man with red hair?" she asked in a whisper, and he nodded as he set about saddling the mare which was Charmian's usual mount.

"Miles was too damned careless to make sure it remained undiscovered," he said. "Too careless, or too cocksure! Believe me, m'dear, our race here is run! I can see that, if Miles and Lavinia cannot, and I've made my plans accordingly. Once you are safe at Wychwood, I am taking Amy and the boy and leaving while I am still free to do so, for I doubt whether even my father's ingenuity can save the situation now."

She studied him with puzzled eyes. "Surely any delay must increase your danger," she said diffidently. "Why are you risking their safety, and your own, just to help me?"

He shrugged, apparently intent upon the saddle-girths. "We owe you something for bringing the boy safe home that day. That is Amy's feeling, at all events, and I'll not deny she has been plaguing me to help you. Besides—oh, confound it! Perhaps I am not quite such a scoundrel as I thought I was. Miles is a merciless young devil, and I would always have been plagued by the thought that I could have saved you from him, and did not." He finished saddling the mare, and paused, fondling the animal as he looked across at Charmian with a strange expression in his eyes. "Oh, the devil! You had best know the truth. Miles murdered your father."

She caught her breath and pressed a hand to her lips, for even though she had suspected this to be the truth, it was a shock to hear it so bluntly confirmed. After a second or two she asked in a shaken whisper: "How?"

"Dunton will have told you how we followed him to your home that night," Harry replied. "We had been there before, and, though your father did not know it, had a key to the garden-door. When we found that he knew the truth, I tried to persuade him not to betray us, but

Miles wasted no time upon words. He stepped close beside him, and shot him through the head before your father realized that he was armed. Then he clasped his dead fingers about the pistol and we made our escape, locking the door behind us." He came out from the mare's stall and turned to pick up the other saddle which, like the first, he had earlier placed ready to hand. Then he paused and looked at Charmian with a more serious expression than she had ever seen in his face. "There are few kinds of villainy I have not had a hand in at one time or another," he said quietly, "but I've no stomach for cold-blooded murder. Twice now I have seen Miles kill a man who was unarmed and defenceless, and he would have killed you with as little compunction as soon as he tired of you, and your fortune was safely his."

Behind him the door swung slowly open, its hinges creaking, and against a background of pearly mist stood the slim figure of Miles himself. Harry dropped the saddle and swung round with a curse, and Charmian shrank back, uttering a little, gasping cry of horror.

"Not 'would', dear brother, 'will'," Miles drawled, stepping into the stable. "Upon my soul, I have yet to hear a more nauseating mixture of sentimentality and hypocrisy upon the lips of any man! So Harry Fenshawe has a conscience, has he? That is a jest indeed!"

Harry, recovering quickly from the shock of his brother's arrival, uttered a short laugh and whipped his sword from its sheath.

"Is it, b'Gad?" he retorted. "Then here's another, damn you! I am no helpless sheep ripe for slaughter! Guard yourself!"

He sprang forward as he spoke, so that Miles was obliged to fall back out of reach to gain time to draw his own weapon, and the doorway was left unguarded. Harry, following him, flung an urgent command over his shoulder to Charmian.

"Take the mare and go, before we have the whole household about our ears! I will settle matters here!"

Charmian, stirred from the numb horror which held her prisoner, obeyed with trembling haste. Backing the mare from her stall, she led her out into the yard, and with the aid of the mounting-block there, scrambled into the saddle. The vicious scrape of steel against steel rang still from the stable as she urged the nervous animal forward, out through the open gate at a reckless pace and along the path which led to the woods and the ford below Wychwood Chase. She felt no compunction for her flight. Harry, vigorous and active, was surely more than a match for his dandified young brother, and in any event she could have done no good by remaining. The noise was certain to rouse the servants, and they would not hesitate to drag her back to the house.

In the treacherously dim light of the stable, the two brothers were fighting with grim concentration. They were evenly matched, though Harry's greater height and length of reach inclined the odds very slightly in his favour, and they had fenced together often enough to have the measure of each other's skill. Even after the sound of Charmian's headlong flight had faded into silence, neither had succeeded in gaining any permanent advantage. Miles, goaded by the possibility of his prisoner escaping, and, in doing so, bringing him to answer for his crimes, fell back a pace, and then another, and his left hand reached out furtively towards a bridle which was hanging against the wall.

Securing a firm grip upon it, he dragged it free and with the same movement slashed its steel and leather across his brother's face. Harry uttered a cry of pain and flung up his hands, the sword falling from his grasp, and

Miles's blade drove viciously into his undefended body. He slid to the ground, and his brother sprang over his writhing figure and, slamming the stained sword back into its scabbard, strode to the stall which housed his favourite grey. He led the horse out without troubling to saddle it, and vaulted on to its back. He needed no one to tell him whither Charmian had fled; there was only one place where she was likely to seek refuge.

Charmian herself, unaware of the fate which had befallen her rescuer, was fleeing in blind panic, and something of her terror communicated itself to the mare. At a headlong gallop she thundered across the park and plunged with scarcely any slackening of pace into the woods, along the grassy ride which had grown so familiar to Charmian by daylight, but where mist and moonlight between them had now wrought a strange transformation. Here, caution compelled Charmian to check her speed, in spite of an overwhelming desire to find herself safely within the stout walls of Wychwood Chase. Then only might this nightmare horror end, and safety and sanity once more take possession of the world.

At length, however, it was borne in upon her that the way seemed unduly long, and that even allowing for the deceptiveness of the misty darkness, she should have reached the ford by now. She reined in the mare and looked anxiously about her, but the trees which loomed hugely through the white, wreathing vapour told her nothing. The woods had closed about her, silent and menacing, and to her disordered fancy it seemed that she might wander in them for ever, as though under the spell of some evil enchantment.

With an effort she shook off the illusion and tried to consider her plight in a practical way. She could not bring herself to turn back towards Bell Orchard, but surely if she rode on she would come eventually to the river. Then she need only to follow it upstream until she reached either the ford or the village, from either of which the road to Wychwood Chase was plain enough. Thrusting out of her mind the uneasy knowledge that the woods were honeycombed with paths and that she might be riding in a circle, she urged her mount forward again.

Presently she was rewarded by a slight lessening of the dimness as the trees thinned out towards an open space, and her spirits rose at this indication that the river lay ahead. Next moment she drew rein with a gasp of dismay, hope perishing in a swift flood of terror.

She had emerged, not on to the river bank, but into a clearing, and before her was the squat bulk of a cottage, the outline of its walls and heavy thatch dimly discernible through the swirling mist, a faint light burning in one of its windows. Charmian sat petrified, her flesh crawling with horror, for she had seen this place before, felt its baleful atmosphere even on a morning of summer sunshine. It was Godsall's cottage, crouched like a beast of prey among the crowding trees, holding dark secrets within its ancient walls.

She could feel the mare beneath her quivering with a terror akin to her own, and was overcome by a sense of blind, panic-stricken despair. Behind her lay Bell Orchard, and Miles, and everything that recapture by him implied, and before her, barring the road to safety, this place of brooding evil which she could not bring herself to pass. Impossible, alone in the eerie, mist-wreathed darkness, to smile at the sinister tales surrounding it. The ordeal of the past week had stretched her nerves to breaking-point, and she could almost imagine that unknown powers had drawn her here, powers against which it was futile to fight.

She had made no sound which could possibly have reached the ears of anyone within the cottage, yet it was with no surprise that she saw the door swing open, heard the hinges shriek like a soul in torment, and glimpsed the hulking figure of a man in the lighted doorway. He spoke a gruff command, and a huge dog shot past him and bounded across the clearing, so that the mare whinnied in terror and shied with a violence which took Charmian unawares. She was flung heavily from the saddle, and, dazed and shaken, heard the sound of receding hoofbeats as her mount bolted across the clearing and into the woods.

Bruised and breathless, but driven by a fear which overcame physical weakness, Charmian began to struggle to her feet, only to find the great dog within a yard of her. It growled deep in its throat and bared gleaming fangs, and she froze into stillness again, certain that the least movement would bring it leaping upon her. Then the man's rough voice spoke again, and he came past the snarling brute and gripped her by the arm, hauling her to her feet.

Helpless in his grasp, she was dragged across the little garden and into the cottage, the dog padding silently after them, and found herself in a shadowy, low-roofed kitchen where a dying fire glowed sullenly on a cavernous hearth. The old woman she had dreaded to see was not there, but to one side of the fireplace Amy Godsall was sitting beside the cradle where slept her little son, and the commonplace sight of young mother and sleeping child did something to dispel Charmian's terror of the supernatural. Amy rose slowly to her feet as they entered, staring in astonishment and growing dismay, her eyes wide with silent questioning.

Still holding Charmian by the arm, the man studied her for a moment or two by the light of the tallow candle on the table, and she saw that he had a coarse, brutal face crowned by grizzled, sandy hair. A certain similarity of feature and colouring informed her that this was Jack Godsall, Martha's brother and father to Amy.

"That be the young lady from Bell Orchard," Amy said at last. "Her as Granny brewed the potion for."

"Then how comes she here, alone and at this hour?" Godsall demanded, and tightened his grip on Charmian's arm, twisting it cruelly. "Answer me, drat 'ee! What mischief be ye at?"

Charmian uttered a gasping cry of pain and shook her head helplessly, and with an oath he let her go, thrusting her away so roughly that she fell headlong upon the hearth, avoiding the dying embers by a miracle.

"No need to tell me!" Godsall went on jeeringly. "On your way to the Chase, weren't 'ee, to babble all ye know to Sir Piers? Well, there be a sure remedy for that!"

He spoke curtly to the dog and went out. Charmian started to drag herself up, but the beast growled in warning and Amy said urgently:

"Don't 'ee move, miss, for the love o' pity! He be main fierce, and will heed none but Father." She cast a frightened glance at the door, and added in a whisper: "What went amiss? Where be Harry?"

Charmian shook her head. "I do not know," she murmured. "He released me, but while he was saddling the horses Miles discovered us. They started to fight and I escaped, but lost my way in the woods."

She broke off as footsteps heralded the return of Godsall. He came in carrying a length of rope, with which he lashed Charmian's wrists together in front of her and then fastened the other end of the rope to an iron ring in the inglenook, so that she was held there, half-sitting, half-kneeling on the hearth, her arms outstretched before her as though in supplication. He tested the knots and then stepped back with a nod of satisfaction.

"Seems like they be main careless up at Bell Orchard,

letting 'ee loose like this," he remarked, "but ye'll find as Jack Godsall don't make mistakes o' that kind. Ye'll bide snug here until I know what's to become of 'ee."

He broke off, raising his head to listen, and through the silence came the muffled sound of hoofbeats, rapidly approaching. Amy and Charmian exchanged glances, the thought passing through both their minds that the rider must be Harry. The dog growled softly, and was cursed into silence.

The hoofbeats ceased, and after a moment an imperious knocking fell upon the cottage door. Godsall had not barred it again after bringing Charmian in, and though he moved forward, it screeched open before he reached it and Miles Fenshawe stepped into the room. His glance went quickly from Godsall to his daughter, and then to the bound and huddled figure of Charmian. He laughed softly.

"You are a remarkable fellow, my friend, stap me if you are not!" he drawled. "I come to seek your aid in tracking down a fugitive, and behold! You already have her safely caged. I make you my compliments!"

Before her father could reply, Amy brushed past him to confront Miles. She was wide-eyed and breathless.

"Where be Harry?" she demanded, her voice shrill with anxiety. "What have 'ee done to him? Miss said she left the two of 'ee fighting!"

Miles looked at her, and slowly a smile crept about his lips.

"Why, so we were," he said softly, "and I disarmed him and had him put under lock and key until he comes to his senses. You should thank me for it."

"Thank 'ee for it?" she repeated. "Why should I, when he were trying to save the poor maid yonder from your black schemes?"

Miles laughed. "Was that the tale he told you?" he

drawled. "My poor, deluded Amy, did you suppose that your beauty could cast as potent a spell as her gold? Harry's schemes were the same as my own, save in one small particular. With him, Miss Tarrant would have gone willingly."

"It is not true!" Charmian exclaimed. "If it were, I would not have run away when you began to fight."

"That will not serve," Miles said lazily. "You guessed that I would get the better of Harry, and so you set off for Wychwood to make some wild accusation against me which would keep me out of the way until you and he had left the country. I followed you, but when I came in sight of the Chase and found all dark and silent there, I guessed that you had lost your way. So I came straight here, knowing that if anyone could find you in these woods, Jack Godsall could. I did not expect that you would have been obliging enough to ride up to his door."

"It is not true!" Charmian said again, and twisted round desperately to speak directly to Amy. "You know it is not!"

"Do not let her deceive you, Amy," Miles put in, a note of derision in his voice. "She has been setting her cap at Harry these two years past, though he was shrewd enough to make no response until he could be sure of her fortune. But now he would have deserted you, my dear, you and the child, to go jaunting about Europe, enjoying the riches purchased with a marriage-ring. And there," he pointed to Charmian, "is the cause of it."

"Pay no heed to him!" Charmian cried urgently. "He is trying to trick you—" the words ended in a gasp as Amy stepped forward and dealt her a stinging slap across the face.

"Steal my man, would 'ee?" she said between her teeth. "And I come nigh to helping 'ee do it!" She swung round to face Miles, magnificent in her anger. "Will 'ee take her away, sir? I'll aid 'ee to it, if I can!"

"I'll warrant you will!" he said with a laugh. "Yes, Amy, I will take her away, but there are certain preparations yet to be made. I was on my way to attend to them when I came upon her and Harry making their escape. Keep her for me until I return, and if your grandmother has prepared any more of the potion, be good enough to make her swallow some of it. The less disturbance our departure causes, the better!"

"That I will, sir," Amy replied vindictively. "Granny be sleeping, but I know where she keeps the draught."

"Excellent," he said with satisfaction. "Then I will delay no longer." He looked at Charmian, and made her a mocking bow. "*Au revoir*, Miss Tarrant! Be sure that I shall make all haste to return to you."

He went out, and Godsall, who had listened to all that passed with the sullen taciturnity which seemed normal to him, said abruptly to his daughter:

"'Tis time I were away, too! Leave the wench where she be, and don't let her cozen 'ee into untying her."

"No fear o' that," Amy said savagely. "If Mr Miles don't come back, she can rot there for all I care!"

Godsall nodded and went out, his dog padding at his heels, and Charmian heard the murmur of his voice, and Miles's, in subdued conversation. The baby stirred and whimpered, and Amy hurried to the cradle to soothe him to sleep again.

Charmian bowed her head upon her outstretched arms as tears of weakness and fatigue filled her eyes. She was lost now, more utterly and completely than if she still lay imprisoned at Bell Orchard, for even if, by some miracle, Piers realized that her frantic accusations were true, and came seeking her, he would never think to look for her here. Harry was helpless, and Amy would not help her

now that Miles's poisonous words had done their deadly
work. A sob shook her, and tears splashed down on to
her dusty skirts.

There came a light footstep, a touch upon her shoulder,
and Amy's voice said in a whisper:

"Don't 'ee weep, my dearie! I be main sorry for the
blow I dealt 'ee, but there weren't no help for it!"

Charmian's head jerked up; she said incredulously:
"Then you did not believe him?"

The other girl laid a finger to her lips and slipped away
to the window, where she remained, peering cautiously
out, until they heard Miles ride away. For perhaps a
minute longer she stayed where she was, and then returned to sink to her knees at Charmian's side.

"I know my Harry better nor that," she said with a
smile. "Besides, he couldn't have wed 'ee! He be married
to me."

"To you?" Charmian repeated in astonishment. "But I
do not understand! When were you married?"

"Nigh on three year ago, at a village over Lewes way,"
Amy replied calmly. "There be none knows of it save Father and Harry's own servant, but I be his lawful wife, and
the little lad yonder'll be master o' Bell Orchard one day.
That's why I've held my head so high all this while, even
before Mrs Fenshawe herself." She slipped a hand into
the bosom of her gown and drew out a gold ring hanging
from a slender chain. "Here be the ring Harry set on my
finger on our marriage day! Maybe I'll soon be wearing it
there again."

Charmian stared at her, slowly accepting the truth of
what she said, discovering in it the explanation of so
many things which had puzzled her. Nor was it difficult to
guess the reason for secrecy. No matter how great a rogue
Harry Fenshawe might be, he was well-born and heir to
his father's estate; that he should make Amy Godsall his

mistress offended no one, but in marrying her he had committed an unforgivable sin.

"If the Colonel ever guessed we were wed, he'd cut Harry off in favour o' Mr Miles!" Amy's words seemed to echo Charmian's thoughts. "Harry says as soon as he's saved enough for us to live on, he'll make it known I'm his wife, and damn what the world may say, but"—she smiled again, wryly this time—"seems he be'ant the saving kind!"

"But he meant to take you away from here tonight," Charmian protested. "He told me so!"

"Aye, for 'tis not safe to bide here now. Harry never wanted no part in killing, nor more do I. Lord knows what'll become of us, but anything be better than hanging."

"I will help you," Charmian said impulsively. "You have both been good to me, and nothing can ever repay what you have done." She paused, doubt stirring again in her mind, her eyes anxiously searching Amy's face. "You *will* help me, will you not?"

Amy nodded. "Aye, but we must wait till we be certain Father's not coming back. He's beginning to mistrust Harry, and he half-believed what Mr Miles said just now. I could see it in his face, and if he found I'd set 'ee loose, he'd likely tie me up as well. But he'll be going down to the shore before long, for the lads have work to do tonight."

Charmian correctly interpreted this as meaning that a cargo of contraband was being brought ashore, and realized that it must be Miles's intention to take her aboard the ship that brought it. Aloud she said:

"My horse bolted. How can we reach Wychwood Chase?"

"Father's boat be moored at the foot o' the path. When he be safe away, we'll cross the river and then go up the hill on foot. It be'ant far, if 'ee knows the way." Amy paused and sat back on her heels, considering the situation. "Granny won't wake! I were afeared she might try to stop me going wi' Harry, so I put the potion she brewed for you into the broth I gave her for supper. Reckon she'll sleep till noon."

"The dog?" Charmian spoke anxiously, for the memory of the snarling, fierce-eyed brute was still unpleasantly vivid. Amy shook her head.

"Gone wi' Father. It be trained to give warning if there be strangers about—more reason for us to bide our time! I'd best come with 'ee to Sir Piers. He be the only one likely to help me now, for I dursn't stay here, nor show my face at Bell Orchard."

"He *will* help you," Charmian said with conviction. "You will be safe in his house, until Harry comes for you."

Amy nodded, but absently, as though her attention were elsewhere. She got up and went to the door, opened it a crack, and stood listening intently.

"Someone be coming," she said after a moment. "On horseback, and riding fast."

Horror clutched coldly at Charmian's heart. "Miles?" she said fearfully. "So soon?"

Amy shook her head. "No, he rode towards the shore, and this be coming from Bell Orchard. Belike 'tis Harry!"

The hoofbeats drew nearer and it seemed to Charmian that more than one horse approached. A score of wild surmises flashed through her mind in the brief time it took the rider to reach the clearing, and then, as Amy threw wide the door, the horses came to a stamping halt and a man's voice cried urgently:

"For the love of God, ma'am, come with me at once! Your husband is dying!"

Charmian heard Amy's gasp, her involuntary, agonized denial, and then the manservant spoke again.

"The grooms found him lying in the stable, run through the body! I've done what I can, and Dr Benfleet is with him now, but he cannot last the night. He is asking for you and the child, so for God's sake, make haste! I have brought a mount for you."

Amy swung back into the room. Charmian's cloak, its fastening broken by Godsall's rough handling, lay on the floor. She snatched it up and cast it about her, then, lifting her child from the cradle, wrapped a fold of the cloak about him. She was running again towards the door when Charmian, rousing herself from shock and dismay, cried out in panic.

"Amy, do not leave me here! For pity's sake, set me free before you go!"

In the doorway Amy paused and looked back. She was deathly pale, and her eyes burned darkly with grief and hatred as she stared at the other girl above the child clutched in her arms.

"Damn 'ee!" she said in a breaking voice. "Harry be dying, and all on your account. I'd not set 'ee free to save 'ee from the Devil himself!"

Paying no heed to Charmian's frantic protests, she dragged the door shut behind her, and a few moments later Charmian heard the horses move off. As long as the sound of their hoofbeats could still be heard she remained motionless, straining her ears, half-believing, even now, that Amy would relent and send the servant back to free her.

At last the heavy silence convinced her that the hope was vain. Terror swept over her, and she struggled wildly to free herself from her bonds, sobbing aloud with rising hysteria. But the rope was new and strong, and Godsall had knotted it with pitiless efficiency, and though it cut into her wrists until the blood came, it yielded not a fraction. She fought against it until exhaustion overcame her and she hung limply there, only the bonds preventing her from sliding to the floor.

Time crawled by—how much time she did not know, for every minute seemed like an hour—and the evil in which those ancient walls seemed steeped pressed like a crushing weight upon her. The candle guttered, the embrs chilled to white ash on the hearth, and the shadows crept closer and closer, as though they were her terror and despair made visible. Too spent to move, she crouched there with her head resting on her outstretched arms, a pathetic, defeated figure entreating the uncaring night for a mercy she could not hope to find. Outside, the mist lay like a shroud over the silent woods, and the river glided, quiet and cold as a snake, towards the sea.

15

Daybreak

Charmian had fallen into a stupor of hopelessness and fatigue, a merciful dulling of the senses from which she was roused at last by the weird shriek of hinges as the door of the cottage was thrust open. Wearily she lifted her head, knowing already what she would see, and watched Miles step into the room. He looked at the deserted kitchen and the empty cradle, and smiled.

"So someone brought the news from Bell Orchard," he said, half to himself. "Well, no matter! I shall be safe out of England tonight."

He strolled across to the fireplace and stood looking down at Charmian, who stared back at him with horrified fascination. It seemed incredible that this was the young dandy whom she had once regarded with tolerant but faintly contemptuous amusement, whose persistent courtship she had found merely tiresome. He looked still as he had always done; the delicately handsome face, the powdered curls, the faultless riding-dress—these were the marks of the exquisite, the man to whom dress and manner were the only things of any real importance. Yet, to her knowledge, he had the blood of three men on his hands, and one of these his own brother. It was grotesque and horrible that evil should appear in so harmless a guise, and she shuddered and shrank away. This seemed to amuse him, for he laughed softly.

"You are not very welcoming, my dear," he remarked mockingly, "and yet one would suppose you eager to be delivered from so uncomfortable a situation. Damme if I ever saw a more dreary hole than this! No wonder the villagers tell such awesome tales of it." He took a penknife from his pocket and began to hack at the rope securing her to the wall. "However, you will soon have seen the last of it! Godsall's boat is ready, and I have brought a sturdy fellow to man it. He will row us downstream and out to the *Pride of Sussex*, which at present lies at anchor offshore, and in this very convenient mist no one will see us go. So there is not the smallest chance that you will evade me again."

The last strands of rope parted, but Charmian was powerless to move, for her wrists were still pinioned together and she was numb and cramped in every limb. Miles lifted her to her feet and held her there, one arm about her waist, while with his other hand he turned her face towards him and studied it searchingly by the light of the guttering candle.

"I have always wanted you," he said reflectively, "and if you had taken the trouble to know me better, you would have realized that what I want, I take, no matter who stands in the way. Your father would not consider your marriage with a younger son; Rob Dunton risked his life to tell you the truth about me; Harry tried to place you beyond my reach. All three are dead, or dying!"

Charmian stared, fascinated and repelled, at the handsome face so close to her own. Her mind seemed as numb and powerless as her body, but slowly one thought took shape, bringing with it a kind of bitter thankfulness. Of the men who had tried to save her, Piers at least had escaped unharmed; she was beyond his protection now, but she would cling to that small shred of comfort, the only one left to her in this hour of utter despair.

Miles's hold upon her tightened, he bent his head and kissed her lingeringly upon the lips, but she was beyond feeling now, and lay inert as a dead woman in his arms. Her lack of response infuriated him, and he thrust her away and into the chair beside the cradle. There was an evil expression in his eyes.

"Still so damned indifferent?" he said viciously. "No matter! I will teach you otherwise once we are safe away from here."

He jerked a handkerchief from his pocket and tied it tightly across her mouth with a callousness which betrayed the ugliness of his mood. Then he gripped her arm and heaved her to her feet, forcing her across the room and out through the open door. The first grey glimmerings of dawn were in the sky and the grass beneath their feet was heavy with dew, but the mist still lay white and ghostly over a sleeping world. Charmian tripped on her trailing skirts and nearly fell, and with a muttered curse Miles hoisted her up across his shoulder, and, thus burdened, went on across the clearing and down the winding path to the river.

Borne thus unceremoniously, Charmian could see nothing, but now and then wet leaves brushed her face, and she could smell the damp, earthy scent of the woods. Then the quiet lap and gurgle of water reached her ears, and it seemed to her overwrought imagination that the river was chuckling to itself in soft, sinister mockery of her helplessness.

Miles set her on her feet again, supporting her with one arm, and she saw the dim shape of a boat against the misty glimmer of the stream, and the figure of the man seated in it. He sat with bent head, his elbows resting on his knees, his face hidden in the shadow of a shapeless hat, and the white of his shirt, for he wore no coat, a patch of lighter colour in the dimness.

"Jem!" Miles said curtly. "Good God, man! are you asleep? Bestir yourself and take the lady from me!"

The man rose slowly, balancing himself in the gently rocking boat, and Miles thrust Charmian into his out-stretched arms. These received her gently and closed about her with a curious sense of comfort, and though she could not see his face, a wild, incredulous suspicion awoke within her, kindling a tiny, tentative flicker of hope. Surely she had been held thus before, only yesterday, in an embrace at once strong and tender? Either she was mad indeed, or the man now holding her was Piers him-self.

He laid her down in the stern of the boat and turned again towards Miles, but something in his appearance or manner aroused the other man's suspicions and he drew back, his hand going swiftly to his pocket.

"What trickery is this?" he said sharply. "You are not Jem Channock!"

Piers, reading correctly the purpose of the movement, wasted no time in affirming or denying this, but with a leap which left the boat rocking wildly, flung himself ashore and grappled with Miles before the pistol could be brought into play. They crashed together to the ground, and Charmian, from her lowly position in the boat, could see nothing of the ensuing struggle, and could only judge of its violence by the sounds which reached her.

Miles, balked thus on the very brink of success, fought viciously in spite of being at a considerable disadvantage. He had no liking for the more brutal forms of combat, and not only was Piers larger and stronger than he, but he had been uppermost when they fell. Miles was shaken and breathless, but, urged on by the certainty that defeat would mean not only the loss of Charmian and her fortune, but imprisonment and execution, he gave a good account of himself.

He would not have hesitated to use the pistol, but it had been knocked from his hand by the shock of the fall and was lost somewhere in the undergrowth, but as he struggled to free himself from Piers' grip, another weapon presented itself. The fingers of one hand, groping blindly across the ground, came in contact with a large stone half buried in the earth; he wrenched it loose, and struck with all his remaining strength at his opponent's head. The blow was a lucky one. Piers uttered a grunt and became suddenly limp, and Miles, thrusting his inert body aside, rose shakily to his feet.

He staggered to the water's edge and clambered into the boat, and Charmian uttered a moan of desolation. So her fate remained unaltered, and Piers had not, after all, escaped unscathed. She would never know, now, what had befallen him, and could only pray silently that he had escaped with his life.

Miles's movements were clumsy and he was breathing heavily. He had lost his hat, and his powdered wig was tilted rakishly over one eye, but there was nothing laughable in his appearance as he fumbled to loose the boat from its moorings. Even his victory over Piers could not soothe the viciousness of his mood, for he dare not stay to discover what had become of Jem Channock, and must make swift to row the boat himself. He had learned as a boy to handle the oars, and they would be travelling with and not against the stream, so there was little risk of not reaching the ship, but this was not at all as he planned it. Thanks to Piers Wychwood, he must now appear ridiculous to the captain and the crew of the *Pride of Sussex*, and the knowledge roused him to a simmering hell of fury.

Piers himself had been only momentarily stunned. He came dizzily back to consciousness, and then, as recollection returned, dragged himself to his knees in time to see Miles casting off from the river bank. Knowing that it was the last, slim chance of saving Charmian, and spurred by that knowledge to supreme effort, he stumbled to his feet and launched himself desperately across the widening strip of water.

He landed anyhow in the boat, which rocked perilously under the impact, and Miles cursed and flung himself at him again. As the little craft, caught by the strong current, was carried towards midstream, the two men fought desperately for supremacy. The boat pitched and rocked beneath their shifting weight, and water splashed into it, but neither paid any heed. Only Charmian, bound and helpless in the stern, realized the inevitability of disaster, and she could not cry a warning because of the gag about her mouth. Beyond fear and beyond hope, she watched the boat tilt farther and farther, and then water rushed over the gunwale and it capsized. She heard one of the men give a yell of terror, and then, as chill, black water closed over her head, her senses left her.

Her first sensations, when she again became aware of anything at all, were of cold and extreme discomfort, and then she realized that she was lying upon grass, the gag was gone from her mouth, and someone was loosening the last strands of rope from about her wrists. Vivid in her memory was the last scene upon which she had looked, and, fearfully, she opened her eyes, but it was Piers who was kneeling beside her. She whispered his name, and he caught her up in his arms, holding her tightly as though he could never bear to let her go.

"Piers!" she sobbed. "Oh, Piers, I was so frightened!"

"I know, my little love, I know!" he murmured. "But it is over now, thank God, and you are safe!"

She knew that this was true, but the ordeal had been so prolonged and her despair so absolute, that she could not yet wholly believe that she had escaped it. Pressing closer to him, and looking fearfully about her, she whispered questioningly: "Miles?"

Piers shook his head. "He could not swim," he replied quietly, "and my only thought was to bring you safely ashore. He had no hope of escaping."

Charmian looked at the faintly glimmering water sliding past close beside them, with white trails of mist drifting like ghosts across its surface, and felt a shiver not wholly due to the clammy chill of her wet clothes. Miles had deserved death; if Piers could have made him prisoner it would have been merely the first step along a road leading inevitably to the gallows, but it would be a long while before she could forget the manner of his passing.

"I do not understand," she said faintly. "How did you come to be in the boat? It was like a miracle!"

"It was no miracle, dear heart! I approached the cottage from Bell Orchard as Miles reached it from the other direction, and I heard him tell you he had brought a man with him to row you out to the ship. I realized that I must somehow dispose of the fellow and take his place, for I had to get you away from Miles before making any move against him. I could not risk his using you as a hostage."

Still not fully comprehending, she would have questioned him further, but he laid his hand gently upon her lips.

"All the rest can wait," he said firmly. "It is far more important that you should be properly looked after, and the sooner I get you into my mother's care, the better it will be."

He got up and helped her to her feet, and for a few

moments held her close as she leaned weakly against him. After a little she looked up into his face, uttering a little cry of alarm at seeing it darkly streaked with blood.

"Piers, you are hurt!" she exclaimed in dismay. "I did not know!"

He lifted a hand to his forehead and then glanced at the red stain on his fingertips. "It must look a deal worse than it is," he said ruefully, "for I had forgotten it. Forgive me, Charmian! I did not mean to frighten you. Believe me, 'tis little more than a scratch!"

She was not altogether reassured, but said no more, realizing that the longer they delayed, the longer his injury must wait for the attention which she was convinced it needed. Only, when he would have lifted her to carry her up the hill, she shook her head, saying shakily but with determination:

"It is too far! I am sure I can walk, if you will help me a little."

He let her have her way, hoping that movement would do something to dispel the effects of cold and shock, for she was shivering violently, and he was himself aware of the discomfort of wet clothes and the chilliness of the air. It was high summer, but in that grey, misty hour before sunrise the world seemed drained of warmth as it was of colour. So side by side they set off up the hill, and Charmian struggled resolutely on until they reached the foot of the steps leading to the lowest of the three terraces below the house, though she stumbled with increasing frequency, and leaned ever more heavily upon Piers' arm. The sight of the broad flight of steps sweeping upwards, however, and the knowledge that two more flights lay beyond it, conquered her determination, and she said faintly:

"I am sorry, but I cannot . . . walk any farther."

"It does not matter, my dear!" Piers looked down at

the drooping figure beside him, aware of a deep thankfulness that she was safe at last in the protection of his home. Then he lifted her in his arms, and slowly, for he was very tired, began to climb the steps towards the house.

Miss Dorothy Wychwood, sunk in that blissful slumber of which not even profound anxiety could rob her, was rudely startled out of it by some sound which, on waking, she could not immediately define. As she lay staring perplexedly before her, it came again, a sharp, rattling noise from the direction of the window, as though someone had flung a handful of earth against the glass.

Wide awake now, she sprang out of bed and padded barefoot across the room to throw curtains and window wide. In the east, the sky was flushing faintly pink with the coming dawn, but a thick carpet of mist lay upon the ground, so that trees and shrubberies, their bases hidden, seemed to float mysteriously upon it like ships upon a milky sea. Below her, she could make out the figure of a man, who, as she leaned from the window, spoke in a tone of muted urgency.

"Dorothy!" It was her brother's voice, hoarse with weariness. "Come down and open the door. I've no wish to rouse the servants."

Astonished but willing, Dorothy waved assent and drew back into the room, fumbling for wrap and slippers. Dragging these on, she opened the door and stole softly downstairs, wondering what had possessed Piers to arrive home at this unreasonable hour, and why, having done so, he desired to be admitted with such stealth to his own house. Such erratic behaviour was totally unlike him.

In the wide hall, grey with the dawn-light filtering through the tall windows, she struggled with bolts and chains. They yielded at last and she pulled open the door, to recoil with a squeak of astonishment at the sight which met her eyes.

On the threshold stood Piers—practical, unadventurous Piers—hatless and coatless, blood trickling down his face from a cut on his brow where a great bruise was also beginning to darken, and his clothes oozing water. He was carrying Charmian. Her arms were clasped about his neck and her face hidden against his shoulder, and water dripped from her tangled hair and from the bedraggled gown which clung in sodden folds about her. While his sister stared disbelievingly, Piers brushed past her into the hall, saying calmly:

"Lock the door again, and come with me."

As in a dream, Dorothy obeyed, wordless for once with amazement, and followed him up the stairs to her own room. There Piers set Charmian down in a chair, murmured something to her that his sister could not catch, and then straightened up, adding briefly:

"Look after her, Dorothy! I will fetch our mother."

He went out, and Dorothy, consumed with curiosity and excitement, hastened across to her friend, but Charmian was shivering and sobbing, plainly on the point of collapse, and it was obvious that explanations would have to wait. When circumstances demanded it, Dorothy could be as practical as Piers himself, and by the time that Lady Wychwood came hurrying in, she had Charmian out of her wet clothes and into her own warm bed, and was standing beside her, holding her hand and staring in horror at the red, raw mark of the rope about her wrist.

"Mama!" she whispered in a stricken voice as her mother reached her side. "Look at this!"

Lady Wychwood uttered a shocked exclamation, and bent over Charmian to lay a gentle hand on her forehead, smoothing back the damp, tumbled hair.

"My poor child!" she said tenderly. "Piers has told me something of what you have been through, and be sure that we shall take great care of you, now that we have you safe."

Charmian had reached that point of utter exhaustion where, now that she was warm and comfortable at last, sleep could no longer be held at bay, but Lady Wychwood's words penetrated her fading consciousness. With a tremendous effort she forced her eyes open again, and said huskily:

"He is hurt! He said it was nothing, but I am not sure. I am very well now, so please look after Piers."

Her eyelids drooped again, and she scarcely heard Lady Wychwood's reassuring answer as she sank into unfathomable depths of sleep. Her ladyship stood for a moment looking down at her, and then, becoming brisk, sent Dorothy to fetch salves and bandages so that she might dress the injured wrists. While she did so, she passed on to her daughter such information as Piers had given her concerning the events of the night, though this was scanty, and did little to satisfy their curiosity. They would not know the full story for some hours yet.

Piers, meanwhile, had gone from his mother's rooms to his own, and summoned his valet, an imperturbable, elderly man upon whose discretion he could depend. There were many things yet to be done, but he must take a few hours rest before setting about them, and having permitted the servant to dress the cut on his forehead, and issued instructions that he was to be awakened before the morning was too far advanced, he flung himself wearily into bed. For the time being he could do no more.

He was up and out again by midday, and his business kept him away from the Chase until late afternoon. When he returned he went first to speak to his mother, whom he found in the smaller drawing-room. He greeted her with his customary courtesy, but added immediately:

"How is Charmian?"

"She is beginning to recover," Lady Wychwood replied. "I sent for Dr Benfleet, and he is of the opinion that a few days of rest and quiet will repair the physical effects of her recent experiences, though I fear it will be long before the poor child forgets what she has been through. He advised me to keep her in bed, but she seems greatly troubled by some matter which she will not confide to me, and says only that she must talk to you. She was growing agitated, and so I allowed her to get up on condition that she remained resting on the couch in my dressing-room, and promised to go back to bed as soon as she has spoken with you."

Piers frowned. "Did she give you no hint of what is troubling her?"

"None at all. I thought that it might be on account of Harry Fenshawe, for she reproaches herself bitterly that he suffered through trying to help her, but Dr Benfleet was able to tell us that he now has a good chance of recovery."

"Yes, that is so," Piers agreed absently. "I have been to Bell Orchard. All is in confusion there, but at least it seems probable that Harry will live. I cannot help but be glad of it."

"Nor I," Lady Wychwood said gravely, "but, Piers, is it true that that foolish young man is married to Amy Godsall?"

"Quite true!" He looked quizzically down at her. "I can see, ma'am, that you, like the rest of the world, will never forgive him, but for my part, I must confess that in some ways I admire him for it."

"Well, we will not quarrel on that score," his mother replied with a smile. "There is a great deal that I would like to ask you, but it will wait until after you have seen Charmian. Go up to her now, my dear, for she will not rest until she has talked to you, and I do not wish her to become too tired. You will find Dorothy with her."

As Piers approached the dressing-room, he heard his sister chattering eagerly within, though her voice ceased abruptly when he knocked. Her light footstep approached the door, and she opened it, to exclaim delightedly:

"Piers, at last!" She stood aside for him to enter, and followed him across to the couch where Charmian was lying, adding frankly: "Well, you look a great deal more presentable than you did when last I saw you, in spite of that bruise on your forehead. I was never more astonished in my life than I was when I opened the door this morning."

He ignored this comment and took the hand Charmian put out to him, saying with a smile: "Are you feeling better? My mother says there is something you wish to tell me."

"Yes, there is," she replied hesitantly, and looked dubiously at Dorothy. "I fear Lady Wychwood found my insistence tiresome, but truly, it is very important."

"I am sure it is," he replied reassuringly, "and I imagine that you would prefer to discuss it with me alone."

"I," Dorothy informed him pointedly, "am here as chaperone. However, if you will both undertake to stand by me when Mama takes me to task—" she left the sentence unfinished, and with an airy gesture tripped out of the room. Piers watched the door close behind her, and then turned back to Charmian.

She lay propped against a pile of cushions, wearing one of Dorothy's gowns in a soft shade of blue, with her hair uncovered and very simply dressed. She still looked pale and ill, with dark shadows beneath her eyes, and some haunting trouble in the eyes themselves, and he realized that the grim menace of Bell Orchard had not yet been entirely dispelled. The hand she had put out to him in greeting still rested in his, and now he sat down beside her on the couch and took the other hand also in a firm clasp, saying gently:

"What is it, my dear? What is troubling you?"

"Something that Harry told me last night," she said in a low voice. "Piers, Miles murdered my father! He shot him while he was unprepared and defenceless, just as he killed the Jacobite a few days ago." She paused, her fingers clinging tightly to his as though finding strength and comfort in the contact. "I do not know how much I told you when you came to Bell Orchard the other day, for my memory of that time is still confused, but it is all clear in my mind now. I can tell you everything that happened."

She did so, her soft, hesitant voice recounting a tale of greater and more tortuous villainy even than he had imagined. When she had done, he sat for a little while without speaking, but at last he said quietly:

"Miles should have hanged, but he is beyond the reach of justice now. They found his body this morning. As for Colonel Fenshawe, I imagine that he has made his escape, for when Mrs Fenshawe discovered last night that you had fled, she summoned her coach and set off as fast as she could for London. Had I not ridden cross-country, I would have met her on the road, but it is too late to pursue her now. There remains only Harry."

"That is what troubles me," Charmian said anxiously. "It was Colonel Fenshawe who schemed to rob my father, and Miles who murdered him and the other man. I know that Harry aided them, but he did his best to make amends, and it does not seem just that he should be left to bear the punishment alone. He and Amy tried to help me, and have already suffered because of it. I do not want them to suffer more."

He regarded her curiously. "Even though Amy left you, bound and helpless, to await Miles's return?"

Charmian nodded. "Even so," she replied quietly. "Oh, Piers, how can I bear her a grudge for that? She loves Harry, and believed that he had lost his life through helping me. I think that, in her place, I would have done the same."

"It is true," Piers said slowly, "that but for her, I would not have known where to find you. When I reached Bell Orchard and found that you had disappeared, and that neither Miles nor Mrs Fenshawe was in the house, I made them take me to Harry's room. He was unconscious, but Amy told me where you were, and what Miles was planning to do. Had she not done so, I could not have arrived in time."

"Then can we not find some way of helping them? I do not know how much of all this must be made known, but at least only you and I know that Harry was present when his brother committed murder." She paused, her eyes anxiously searching his face, and then added pleadingly: "Would it be very wrong for us to keep silent?"

Piers did not reply at once, but he knew already that he was going to do as she asked. This was not simply to please her, to see the trouble and anxiety vanish from her eyes, although this was the most compelling reason. He found that he could not forget the old bond of friendship between himself and Harry, or the debt of gratitude he owed to him and to Amy. She, too, had a right to be considered; as Harry's wife her position would be difficult enough, but as his widow it would be intolerable.

"Right or wrong," he said at length, "that knowledge we will share with no one. Harry and Amy have trouble enough already."

"He consorted with the Jacobites," Charmian said

doubtfully. "Does that not mean he would be held guilty of treason?"

Piers shook his head. "You forget," he said with a faint smile, "that I still lack proof of that. There was nothing to connect that poor fellow Miles killed with the Stuarts, and I can promise you that no more mysterious strangers will come ashore from the *Pride of Sussex*. I have spoken to Jack Godsall, and he knows that in his treatment of you last night I have a weapon against him which I shall not hesitate to use if he gives me cause. In future he will confine his activities to ordinary smuggling, and he is likely to find that less easy and profitable now that Fenshawe is no longer here to bribe the Excisemen. As for Harry, I do not know whether it will be possible to save him altogether from the consequences of what he has done, but I give you my word that I will do my best, and if the worst happens, and he is imprisoned, I will see that Amy and the child are cared for. Will that content you?"

She nodded, and gave a tremulous smile. "You are very good," she said unsteadily, "and I owe you so much! I still do not know exactly how you came to be at the cottage last night. Dorothy said she thought you had gone to Richmond."

"I did go there," he replied, "and what I learned from your friends told me that your danger was even greater than I had supposed. I came straight back to Bell Orchard, but you were no longer there."

Charmian looked puzzled. "How did you discover that?" she asked. "Surely they did not tell you!"

"They had no choice!" Piers spoke calmly, but there was a gleam of rueful laughter in his eyes. "I was in no mood by then to be denied, and when the servants tried to turn me away, I regret to say that I forced my way into the house at pistol-point." He laughed softly. "They were so astonished at my behaviour that they told me the truth straightway, and even showed me your empty room in proof of it. Then Amy told me where to find you, and the rest you know."

Charmian smiled also, but there was more than amusement in her eyes. "I should have had more faith in you," she murmured. "Dorothy has explained it all to me now, but when you left me at Bell Orchard the other day, when I had pleaded so desperately for your help, I thought that you did indeed believe me mad. I am ashamed now at my lack of trust."

Piers lifted her hand to his lips. "You must not be," he said gently, "but there is a memory which shames *me*, and that is the readiness with which I believed Miles's lies about you. Did Dorothy tell you of that also?"

Charmian nodded, and a shadow darkened her eyes again. "He was very clever," she said in a low voice, "and very ruthless. There was nothing in the world that mattered to him, except himself."

"He was always so, even as a boy," Piers agreed quietly. "If I had remembered that, you would have been spared so much. It will be long before I forgive myself for my blindness." He paused, regarding her with a troubled frown. "I wish that your rescue could have been more prosaically accomplished. Whatever we do, there is bound to be a deal of talk."

"More gossip!" Charmian said with a sigh. "First in London, and now here!" She looked wistfully up at him. "What ought I to do?"

"I have been thinking about that," he replied. "Mr and Mrs Brownhill are on their way here, and I believe that, when you are stronger, it will be best if you return with them to Richmond. By the time you are out of mourning, all this will be forgotten."

A week before, a return to Richmond had been Charmian's dearest wish, but now the prospect had lost much of its appeal. She had hoped for something other than practical and common-sense advice, and to her dismay she felt tears of weakness and disappointment rising to her eyes. Hoping desperately that he would not see them, she turned her head away, and said in as steady a voice as she could command.

"Yes, no doubt that *will* be best. My continued presence in this neighbourhood could only be an embarrassment to—to everybody."

"It would be nothing of the kind," Piers said calmly, "but you suffered a terrifying ordeal at Bell Orchard, and that will fade more quickly from your memory when your surroundings no longer remind you of it." He paused, smiling a little as he studied her averted face. "I would not let you go, you know, without good reason, and I shall continue to use every endeavour to persuade you to return." He leaned forward, resting one hand on the back of the couch, while with the other he turned her face towards him, adding gently: "Will you, Charmian? I wish so very much to marry you."

The tears were still in her eyes, but now they were tears of happiness. She blinked them away, and shyly lifted her hand to touch his cheek.

"I believe I fell in love with you that night in London," Piers went on, "though the possibility of such a thing was so far from my mind that it was weeks before I knew what ailed me. When I did realize it, I was afraid to tell you, thinking it too soon after your father's death. Perhaps, even now, the time to speak of it has not come, but, truth to tell, I can keep silent no longer. Once already I have come too near to losing you!"

She smiled, looking at him with shining eyes. "Must I find words to tell you what is in my heart?" she whispered. "Oh, Piers, dear love, do you not know?"

He kissed her then, and Charmian, enfolded in his

arms, knew with quiet certainty that the horror of the past few days would slowly fade. One day she would even be able to look with untroubled eyes upon the house at Bell Orchard, though for the rest of her life the worst nightmare which could afflict her would concern an ancient, evil cottage, a rope in the chimney corner, and the uncanny screech of rusty hinges as the door was thrust open. But that would be the dream, the dying echo of terror and despair, and with Piers beside her she would not be afraid. Dreams passed, and were forgotten, but this was the awakening to glad reality.